High on Adventure II

For David & Rosie

Dreams
Becoming
Reality

by Stephen L. Arrington

Huntington House Publishers

Huntington House Publishers
P.O. Box 53788
Lafayette, Louisiana 70505

Library of Congress Card Catalog Number 95-081878
ISBN 1-56384-115-0

Printed in the U.S.A.

Dedication

Written with love for my wife, Cynthia Elizabeth Arrington, who loves challenges, tackles adventure with enthusiasm, and courageously pursues the wonder of life.

A new command I give you: Love one another. As I have loved you, so you must love one another. By this all men will know that you are my disciples, if you love one another.

—John 13:34

A dream is a wish your heart makes.

—Cinderella

Cover artwork and story illustrations
by Margery Spielman

Contents

Introduction

To be content with mediocrity is a tragedy.
—Ruth Smeltzer

Most opportunities in life are created by active pursuit.

High on Adventure II is about life quests. How exciting and fulfilling our lives will be is mostly self-determined. The keys to a dynamic future are attitude, commitment, discipline, and the courage to pursue achievable dreams. We have the power to choose an imaginative path that can lead to challenge, wonder, and adventure. Along the way we can experience incredible love, enjoy long-term happiness, and savor the satisfaction of a good life well spent.

Sadly, many people actively choose to live uninspired lives. I say *actively choose* because this is a conscious decision they continually make on a daily basis. They willfully allow the treadmill of a mediocre life to carry them haphazardly into an uneventful future.

When a person's existence seems to lack meaning, it usually leads to depression and sometimes to anger. A person can always reverse negative trends though positive choices. Unfortunately, some individuals instead will slip in an even worse direction. They will purposefully decide to make poor, or even bad, choices that can take them on a dark journey to evil places. I know, because I have been to the shadow lands. It certainly was not my intent to journey into darkness; the mistakes, at first, seemed so small . . .

In the shadow lands there is no happiness or love. It is an evil place full of pain where fear is a constant companion. The errors that led me into that dark underworld were my own.

However, it is important to know that if a person makes a mistake it does not mean that *person* is a mistake. Amazing grace they call it. What I have learned about the power of good choices is the theme for *High on Adventure II*.

> Take my yoke upon you and learn from me, for I am gentle and humble in heart, and you will find rest for your souls. For my yoke is easy and my burden is light. (Matt. 11:29-30)

The foundation of this book is built on a simple fact. Living an active Christian lifestyle is the best path to adventure, wonder, love, and extraordinary happiness.

One

Life is a pretty precious and wonderful thing. You can't sit down and let it lap around you. You have to plunge into it; you have to dive through it!

—Kyle Crighton

It is hot, really hot. The *Alcyone's* deck simmers under the blazing Australian sun. In my silver wet suit, I feel a lot like a foil-wrapped baked potato. Rivulets of sweat run down my legs, adding to the substantial puddles already inside my rubber booties. I stare anxiously at the cool ocean water as I strap on a heavy lead weight belt, then buckle on a second one for added underwater stability. I won't be wearing fins for this dive, nor will I be doing any swimming (that is, unless something goes terribly wrong). Swimming in shark-infested water is not generally considered a good idea—particularly when the predators in question are large, hungry, great white sharks.

Shouldering a silver scuba pack, I begin moving ponderously toward the stern of the Cousteau Society's wind ship. The open hatch of a floating shark cage bobs lightly in the calm water. Sunlight on the glassy surface ripples and sparkles in open invitation.

"Can't you waddle any faster?" urges Capkin. The tall, lean Australian is anxious to go below to the dining salon. His nose flares as he sniffs at lunch-time smells wafting through the open door of the bridge. Capkin's first concern always centers around his stomach.

"I don't know how you can get so excited about fish-head soup," I reply, spitting into my dive mask to keep it from fogging up in the cold water.

"Only real men eat fish-head soup," grins Capkin, pounding his chest for emphasis. He is sporting the beginning of a new beard. His white teeth gleam brightly from the shadow of dark stubble.

The soup in question has been simmering on the stove all morning. I had mistakenly lifted the lid in hopeful pursuit of oatmeal and looked inside. I still couldn't shake the memory of those empty fish eyes staring back from a slimey, yellow, bubbling broth.

"Would you mind making me a peanut butter and jelly sandwich on whole wheat?" I ask hopefully.

"Bruno isn't going to be impressed," laughs Capkin. Our French chef has a low opinion of peanut butter, catsup, corn flakes, and other such American staples. I often bait him by adding assorted condiments to my peanut butter sandwiches, such as potato chips, bananas, figs, raisins, honey, and an occasional cucumber.

"Throw in a pickle," I grin. "That ought to fire him up."

Picking up a Nikonos underwater camera, I suddenly remember the last sandwich Capkin made for me. "Say, Capkin, this time could you check the cutting board for fish slime and scales before making my sandwich, OK?"

Abruptly, a large gray fin surfaces and knifes through the water just a few feet from the swim step.

"Speaking of fish scales," observes Capkin, "Murf's back."

The great white shark's head lifts out of the water and glares in our direction. No light reflects from its dark pupil. The stare is cold and predatory. I watch the fifteen-foot-long superpredator glide silently beneath the stern of the wind ship.

Despite the muggy heat of the day, a chill of anticipation runs down my spine.

"You know my dad always said it is better to eat the fish than to be eaten by the fish," confides Capkin over my shoulder.

"That's reassuring," I answer, wondering if Murf has brought any toothy friends. "Mind pulling the cage a little closer?"

A couple of seconds later I jump through the open hatch of the floating shark cage. Cold water immediately floods my wet suit, but I hardly notice as I see Murf swimming eagerly in my direction. Apparently the shark thinks it's his lunch time, too. I'm thankful there are some high-quality steel bars between me and the oncoming eating machine. Murf impacts the cage nose first—which cannot feel very good. He hits the solid steel bars a second time, then shakes his muzzle like a boxer trying to recover from a head blow. Obviously, Murf isn't a very bright fish.

A moment later, Capkin's large foot pushes against the top of the cage, shoving it out into the tidal current. While waiting for the cage to drift to the full length of its twenty-foot tether, I find it momentarily amusing that this little experiment is my own idea.

Like most fish, great white sharks actually tend to be rather shy around people. The chances of a person being attacked by a shark are only about one in fourteen million. The odds are much better, by a factor of ten, for someone to be struck by a lightning bolt. Hanging out with great white sharks in South Australian waters does increase my odds a bit, particularly since we've been chumming the water with fish parts and dried blood, which tends to get the sharks rather excited—also known as a feeding frenzy.

So far we have encountered only a few great whites and they have mostly kept their distance. I figure that by being the only one in the water, and with no one on the deck of the *Alcyone* to distract them, I might actually be able to lure the sharks in closer. Capkin calls my unique idea the human bait approach. I hopefully wave a dead tuna at Murf, but he just swims away. In the realm of great white sharks, Murf is rather timid.

Slowly the minutes pass as I stare idly at the empty water. Glancing at the black steel bars about me, they stir distant memories that slowly solidify.

Mentally traversing the corridors of my mind, the steel bars take on a more sinister look. They remind me of other steel bars, but these were not for my protection. No, they were meant to keep me inside. My prison cell was slightly larger than the dimensions of a shark cage, yet it represented a lot less freedom.

My sojourn in prison was a long time ago; it began with a single marijuana cigarette. First, I used marijuana; then I agreed to sell a little to a friend. One of the things that I learned in prison was that it is usually friends who encourage us to make negative choices. Drugs, any illegal drugs, corrupt our morals and the way we think. Because of marijuana, I became one of those people—the friend who was willing to lead another astray.

At first, I argued that it wasn't I who was forcing them to use the drug; yet, it was I who was making it available. I was not taking any responsibility for my actions. I successfully avoided that until I wound up in a prison cell—then I couldn't avoid my own accountability any longer.

While I was in prison, I realized a couple of things that would change my life forever. When we do something wrong, that wrongness binds us. These are chains of our own making. To break the bonds takes two simple steps. First, we must take responsible for our actions. It is only through accepting ownership that the errors can be given away. The second step is realizing that Jesus will forgive our worst behavior. If we make a mistake, it does not mean that we *are* a mistake.

We do not earn our redemption. Fortunately, that means of measurement is not asked of us. Jesus has already decided that we are worth it and He went to the cross to prove it.

> **When God measures a man,**
> **He puts the tape around the heart instead of the head.**
> **—Anonymous**

Because of the Lord's forgiveness, I was able to put my life back together. By actively reading the Bible, I realized that the Ten Commandments do not restrict us; instead, the Lord's laws set us free. By focusing on doing good works, I rediscovered happiness and even went on to realize a childhood dream of diving with the Cousteau Society.

No matter what is wrong with a person's life, God can fix it in an instant, if we let Him.

My thoughts are brought back to the present abruptly when the cage jars and a heavy shutter vibrates up through my feet.

Looking downwards, I see a huge great white shark chewing on the heavy steel mesh at the bottom of the cage. The shark's large chompers are only inches from my rubber-bootied feet. It takes me several heartbeats to realize that this aggressive behavior does not fit Murf's laid-back personality. No, the seventeen-and-a-half-foot-long shark who is industriously going after my toes is Amy! She is a three-thousand-pound great white with a very bad attitude. I quickly swing the underwater camera into action. I see my booties in the frame as Amy torpedoes into the bottom of the cage a second time. The camera catches the shark with her teeth embedded in the steel mesh. Just inches away, my bootied feet are pleased to be a part of the image, but not a part of her lunch.

Speaking of lunch, Capkin delivers mine half an hour later via balloon. It is a rather strange sight, seeing a yellow balloon floating toward you with an odd-looking cargo dangling beneath it. Wrapped inside a clear plastic bag is a very weird sandwich indeed. Snagging the balloon with its unusual baggage, I open the top hatch of the shark cage and climb up into the sunshine to investigate this strange sandwich. What I see is a long bun with a big kosher pickle stuck inside. It looks a lot like a seasick hot dog. Globs of peanut butter, strawberry jelly, and chopped onion leak thickly from the bun.

Capkin and Bruno, the chef, are grinning at me from the stern of the boat. They look quite pleased with their little joke. I find the sandwich intriguing, so I take a mighty bite, which sets Bruno to choking.

"You have no taste," he shouts.

"Anyone who makes fish-head soup has no room to talk," I reply while still chewing. My taste buds find the sharp, contrasting flavors a surprising experience.

"You don't deserve any of my dessert, you weird American." Bruno is holding up a pink balloon with a white ribbon tied to it. Hanging beneath it is a paper party plate inside an inflated plastic bag. He gently places it on the water and pushes it in my direction. The little colorful convoy drifts slowly toward me.

"What is it?" I ask in eager anticipation.

"Peanut butter cheese cake with a raspberry swirl and topped with heavy whipping cream." Bruno is obviously proud of his creation.

Fascinated, I watch the bobbing pink balloon with its dessert baggage. I am mentally wiping the drool from my lips when Capkin casually asks, "Seen any more sharks?"

Without any warning, a two-foot wide mouth shark erupts from the water. Massive teeth chomp down, bursting the pink balloon. A giant tail thrashes wildly, throwing water everywhere; then the shark, and my dessert, plunge beneath the surface.

"That wasn't Murf, was it?" There is water dripping from Capkin's nose. Bruno's waterlogged chef's hat droops to one side. He is speechless.

"No, it's Amy, and she just ate my cheese cake." I quickly duck underwater to see the shark swimming off with a busted pink balloon floating in her wake. Through the sparkling reflection of the surface water, I see Capkin and Bruno rushing off to alert the rest of the crew that we now have a very active shark at the stern of the boat. For a moment, I am a little disappointed to lose my dessert. Then, I realize that there will be other desserts, and this is already sizing up as my most exciting expedition with the Cousteau Society. I check my camera, then peer anxiously into the deep blue water with great anticipation.

> No man is free who is not master of himself.
> —Epictetus

Two

So I saw that there is nothing better for a man than to enjoy his work, because that is his lot.

—Ecclesiastes 3:22

After anticipating an exciting day, I'm let down when nothing significant happens. For several hours, I've been dangling beneath the stern of the *Alcyone* in a clear plastic cage, hoping to attract the attention of a great white shark. Jean-Michel Cousteau wants to see how a great white will react to an apparently cageless diver. Occasionally, I see one begin to approach, but then the shark breaks away and disappears back into the gloom of deeper water.

Glancing over at the steel cinematographer's cage floating twenty feet away, I see Jean-Michel Cousteau, disappointedly signaling an end to the day's diving.

The crew on deck raises the plastic cylinder to the surface so I can scramble out. I am so cold that my fingers are stiff and my movements awkward. Helping hands eagerly pull me out of the water. One of the best aspects of our team effort is the camaraderie. When people labor together, equally sharing in the effort, the work is always easier and the tasks are finished that much faster.

Stripping off my diving gear, I head below for a brief hot shower. Fresh water is always limited on a ship at sea, so I take a sailor's shower. I turn the water on for no more than twenty seconds to soap down and wash off.

Donning sweats, I'm still freezing as I begin my afternoon chores. Every eight days, it is my turn for below-deck duties. I vacuum the carpet, dust the dining salon, clean the bath-

rooms, sweep and mop the kitchen floor, and gather up trash for later disposal ashore. I take my time doing a thorough job of each chore. It is part of an unstated competition. Each crew member knows that if anyone does sloppy work, it will unfairly add to the next person's chores, so all of us try to do a better job than the last person.

Returning to the kitchen, I now have to help Bruno, the chef. I have to set the dinner table and do general kitchen clean-up. Tonight, Bruno is serving beef Wellington, one of his specialty dishes. The filets, which spent most of the day marinating in his secret sauce, are now lightly sautéing in garlic, herbs, and butter. While still hot, Bruno wraps the steaks in dough jackets and puts them in the oven to brown. Meanwhile, he makes another elaborate sauce to accompany the beef Wellington, then adds crumbled bacon to a tray of scalloped potatoes.

"*Voilà*," he announces proudly. "The dinner is ready."

"Yuck," I respond.

"Yuck! What do you mean, *yuck*?" Bruno is outraged. "You crazy American vegetarian. How can you not appreciate my French cuisine?"

"I'm referring to all the pots and pans I have to scrub," I reply tactfully, pointing at the mess in the kitchen.

"It gets worse," Bruno states rather happily considering he is offering bad news. "We're low on fresh water so the engineer doesn't want anyone using the automatic dishwasher."

Later that night, I am again elbow-deep in soapy water washing the dinner dishes when the captain walks up behind me. "You have the mid-watch," he says brightly. This means I have to be up from midnight till 3:00 A.M.

Untying my apron, I rush off to my cabin and, a few hopefully, hours of sleep. Instead, I toss and turn. It seems as if only a moment has passed before a blinding white light is shining in my eyes.

"Time to get up," urges our English sound man.

"OK," I answer, "but stop shining that light in my eyes."

He shrugs, then steps out of the cabin. It does not dawn on him that he has just destroyed my night vision, not a good situation for someone who is about to go on a night watch. The sound man is our audio technician. Having grown up in London's crowded suburbs, he is a city person unaccustomed to being on a ship at sea. The captain only allows him to stand a watch because we are safely at anchor.

Quickly dressing in the dark, I exit the cabin and head for the bridge. The sound man is sitting in front of the radar unit. Its soft greenish light washes across his face as he adjusts the range setting. I notice that there is a slight look of confusion in his eyes.

"Everything OK?" I ask.

"Ugh, yeah," he responds timidly.

I glance at the radar screen. Something looks a little odd about it. Still rubbing the sleep from my eyes, I step outside to inspect the lay of the wind ship. We are anchored a mere tenth of a mile from Dangerous Reef, so I want to check the wind direction and sea state. It is a moonless night, and I am having difficulty seeing anything in the dark. It is then that I notice the deck moving in an oddly rhythmic way. The *Alcyone* is lightly swaying side-to-side, but it doesn't feel like swell-induced motion. The wind ship's deck softly rises as a rushing line of white water passes silently beneath the stern. Quickly looking in the direction of the reef, I see odd-looking florescent splashes of dim light, then I hear the sound of the surf pounding sharp-edged rocks. In alarm, I rush back inside the bridge.

"How far are we from the reef?" I shout.

The sound man immediately panics. "I'm not sure. This radar isn't reading right."

For emergencies, there is a large red button on the bridge. I shove down on it hard. Instantly, the quiet of the night is shattered by the wail of the ship's emergency siren. Moments later, crewmen spill from their cabins in alarm.

"Start up the engines," I yell. "We're almost on the reef."

Christophe, the captain, quickly assumes command. The screws begin turning in less than a minute. The *Alcyone* slowly, and cautiously, maneuvers away from the sharp rocks of Dangerous Reef. It takes an hour to carefully re-anchor the ship.

Christophe is too shook up to sleep, so he offers to take the rest of my watch. As I am leaving the bridge, he quietly confides, "Can you imagine how scary it would be for the *Alcyone* to sink in shark-infested water? At night no less."

I nod, lacking anything important to say.

"If the Englishman wasn't sure how to stand his watch, he should have said something." The captain is mostly talking to himself, yet I answer him anyway.

"It was a mistake," I shrug. "He isn't a sailor."

"No, it's more than that." Christophe fine-tunes the radar. The rotating light bar paints a reflection of the reef's shoreline in soft neon green. A thunderhead falling off several miles to port is shown as an angry smear of bright red light in the upper corner of the scope. "When you tell people that you can do something," Christophe continues, "they rely on you to do it. It's not just that he broke his promise to me, he also endangered everyone aboard this ship."

The captain looks up from the scope; for a moment our eyes meet. "It means I can never trust him again," Christophe says wearily.

In the darkness of my cabin, I lay awake thinking about the sound man. I doubt that he is sleeping either. Maybe his thoughts are clouded with images of dark water and the flashing teeth of great white sharks. Possibly he is thinking about friends struggling to survive in that dark water. Certainly his actions tonight were an accident. He did something he didn't mean to do, yet the bottom line is that he failed us—and himself—in a very big way. Sure, there are many excuses he could offer, but ultimately the responsibility is completely his own.

In the dark cubicle of my cabin, I think about one of my own big mistakes. It landed me in the darkness of a prison cell. Some of the other inmates argued that it wasn't really my fault. Someone that I trusted manipulated me into doing something I didn't want to do. But, the bottom line is that I did do it. And even worse, it wasn't so much that a person manipulated me—it was that they knew they could before they even tried. It meant that this person was aware of my flaws, something I hadn't been willing to face about myself.

Seeing my own faults and realizing how far I had fallen took me down to my knees. In the dim twilight of that prison cell, I realized that none of us is perfect. We are all prone to error. What is important is that we learn to take full responsibility for our actions and determine to make a better choice next time. We can't erase our past blunders, but God can free us of the burden of them (that is the wonder of amazing grace). We certainly don't deserve it. Grace isn't something we can earn; it is a gift freely given.

In the darkness of my cabin, the lingering shadows of my prison experience grow fainter and more distant only because the Lord forgives. I say a quiet prayer of thanks and drift slowly off to sleep.

> Grace and peace to you from God our Father and the Lord Jesus Christ. (1 Cor. 1:3)

Three

Be on your guard; stand firm in the faith; be men of courage; be strong. Do everything in love.

—1 Corinthians 16:13

A heavy swell dramatically lifts the bow of the *Alcyone* then races madly toward the stern. The wind ship's keel slams back down into the raging water, creating a body-shocking shutter that runs the entire length of the hundred-foot hull. Near gale-force winds whip the surface water into frothy waves that beat against the bridge. From inside, I can barely see through the plate-glass windows. Thick rivulets of cascading sea water and heavy rain threatens to overwhelm the window's high-speed wipers. Sitting in the captain's chair, I am quite pleased not to be at sea. Amazingly, the *Alcyone* is taking this beating while tied alongside a pier in Port Lincoln, South Australia, and I am getting seasick—in port!

Most of my friends are astonished that I (a sailor for over twenty years) get seasick. I also find it rather bizarre. It certainly isn't something I enjoy, yet I love being a diver. It is one of the prices I must pay, but in return I have gotten to travel the oceans and to dive in some of the best underwater locations in the world. I just never expected to get seasick while still tied up in the harbor. Fortunately, I am not alone. Standing next to me, Christophe is on the verge of losing his lunch.

"Only an Australian would build a pier in such an exposed place," rages the captain.

We are taking turns adjusting the *Alcyone's* unique turbo sails. These strange-looking metal sails are keeping the wind ship from bashing against the pier. The graceful research vessel strains against the thick ropes that hold it safely in place. A ten-foot gap separates the plunging hull from the steel and cement pier, which would severely damage the *Alcyone* should we accidentally slam against it.

"I'm going below to my bunk," says Christophe, who is looking very pale. Stepping down into the radio room, he doesn't get very far. An instant later, he charges back up and out through the bridge door, throwing himself violently against the side railing. Over the tempest sounds of the raging storm, I hear Christophe choking and gurgling. A minute later, he staggers unhappily back into the pilot house. He is soaking wet from the pounding rain. The captain attempts a feeble grin; then, abruptly, he loses it again—only this time he uses a trash can (the can I had placed beside me, just in case of an unexpected barf emergency of my own). An instant later, I am rushing outside, only I don't quite make it to the railing. Miserably, between gut-wrenching spasms, I stare at the wind ship's wildly plunging deck. Finally, wiping spittle from my chin on Capkin's wet suit (which is conveniently hanging close by), I go back inside, closing the watertight door behind me.

The following morning there is absolutely no sign of the storm. Outside, the sky is deep blue with a few white puffy clouds hugging the horizon. It is very chilly, so I am wearing a thick coat since we are in the midst of the Australian winter. It is early July—not the best month for going out into the Great Australian Bight. The rest of the crew and I are busily loading one last box before getting underway. What it contains is almost as strange as the recent tempest at the seaport.

"So, what's in the box?" Capkin's curiosity is getting the best of him. The huge wooden container is a mystery to the inquisitive divers.

"Something fishy," I reply, playfully dodging the answer.

"That's not much of a hint," complains Antoine. "You're always up to something fishy."

"OK," I grin. "Cindy helped to make it and Capkin will be the first to want to play with it."

Capkin glares at me. He is at the end of his patience. "Tell me what it is or I'll never make you another peanut butter sandwich again."

I instantly give in. "It's a giant toy great white shark."

"Right." Antoine doesn't believe me.

"So open the box," I reply, shrugging my shoulders.

Ten minutes later, the lid of the long box lies on the deck. The crew stares in awe at a twelve-foot-long, mechanical great white shark.

"Jean-Michel wants to see how real great whites will react to Allison," I say while stroking the rubbery latex skin, which looks and feels very realistic. "Allison could answer some questions about whether great white sharks are territorial and how they might react to a strange shark."

We drop anchor at a nearby beach to give Allison a swim test. Jean-Michel wants to check the mechanical shark's buoyancy and swimming ability before putting it into the water with real sharks. While we are suiting up in our dive gear, Capkin sniffs suspiciously at his wet suit. "Smells like someone barfed on my sleeve," he states flatly, looking for the culprit.

"It was Steve." The captain gives me up instantly.

"You barfed on my wet suit?" Capkin is rapidly stripping off the offending rubber suit.

"I only wiped my chin; I didn't barf on it," I answer in my defense. "Besides, I owe you one for the block of cheese you left rotting in my dive bag last expedition."

"That was an accident." Capkin is vigorously plunging the wet suit into a barrel of water.

"Putting a block of cheese in my dive bag was an accident?" I ask, not buying it.

"I thought it was my dive bag." Capkin sniff-checks the suit, then begins putting it on. "I was just packing a snack."

His answer makes sense; Capkin is always hiding food. "Sorry about your wet suit," I offer lamely as I prepare to jump over the side to survey the bottom.

"That's OK," leers Capkin. "Now I owe you one."

Several minutes later, the other divers and Allison join me on the sandy bottom. There is a slight beach surge stirring up the bottom sand and sediment. The back-and-forth movement of the water is creating very gloomy conditions. In the dim, watery light, the mechanical shark looks surprisingly realistic.

Its mouth is half open, revealing twin rows of thumb-sized plastic teeth. Allison's eyes exactly capture the lifeless stare of a real great white shark. She moves slowly through the water, her tail sweeping from side-to-side, propelled by low-pressure air acting against a moveable ram inside the shark's body. The air, piped through an umbilical cord, also maneuvers her pectoral fins for up-and-down mobility. The controls are designed to be operated by a diver inside a steel shark cage. At the moment, Capkin is manipulating Allison's movements.

I am standing on the sand bottom taking pictures of the whole operation when the ballistic arrival of a fur seal pup momentarily captures my attention. Happily watching the playful sea mammal spinning about, I'm a perfect target for Capkin, who seizes the opportunity for revenge. In the dismal water, the mechanical shark's tail begins to move with fiendish purpose.

Looking though my underwater camera's view finder, I follow the antics of the fur seal. Abruptly, the pup stares over my shoulder in alarm, then he dashes off, leaving a wake of frothy bubbles. A sudden impact knocks me off balance. I feel something sharp digging hard into my side. Thinking it is one of the other divers, I quickly look to my left and practically leap right out of my wet suit. A great white shark, its mouth half open, looms before my dive mask. A fright-filled moment slowly passes before I realize it is only Allison. Trying to get my heartbeat back to normal, I look over at the culprit. I can tell that Capkin is giggling by the large cascade of bubbles floating buoyantly out of his regulator.

That night, we re-anchor at Dangerous Reef and begin chumming to attract the sharks. Early the next morning, we launch Allison for real. Murf, the bashful great white, is at the stern and seems to be the perfect candidate for an Allison encounter. It is surprising, and disappointing, when Murf snubs Allison. He could care less about our mechanical shark. Other great whites arrive and still nothing happens; that's when Jean-Michel decides to see how the great whites would react to an apparently injured shark. A small amount of fish blood is pumped into Allison via a plastic hose. The reaction is immediate and comes without warning.

Peaches arrives mouth first. She is an eighteen-foot-long shark with a bite-first-ask-questions-later attitude. The massive predator hits Allison broadside, right in the gills. For a shark, a gill-hit is equivalent to going for the throat (fish breathe through their gills). There is a mighty, loud crunching sound as the thick Lexan plastic bars of Allison's internal frame instantly become rubble.

Confused, Peaches withdraws, spitting out pieces of shredded latex and splintered plastic. Her thought process apparently has only one answer when in doubt. She bites again. It is a really big bite, something that only a great white shark can do with real authority.

At this point it should be noted that great white sharks are not malicious killers. They serve a very important purpose in life. By culling out the weak and the sick, they actually help to keep other marine life healthy. Scavenging the ocean, they also eat dead and decaying animals, which reduces the potential for disease to other marine animals. Great whites mostly seem to act instinctively; they prefer eating things they know and have encountered in the past. When confronted by human beings, they usually, but not always, leave us alone.

The fish blood leaking from Allison fits the great white's profile that this should be lunch, so she takes three more monstrous bites out of the mechanical shark, each time spitting out large quantities of unappetizing Lexan and pieces of latex. Peaches just doesn't seem to realize that there is nothing worth eating here.

For me, the most interesting aspect of this experiment is that the shark is easily biting through Lexan bars that are a full quarter-of-an-inch thick. Please, let me put this in perspective. For the last eighteen months, I have been hanging off the *Alcyone's* stern inside a clear Lexan cylinder (the world's first all-plastic shark cage) to see how great white sharks would react to an apparently cageless diver. The cylinder is made out of three-sixteenths of an inch of Lexan, which is 25 percent thinner than what Peaches is crunching on now. Watching in semishock, I realize that I may have been playing at being an easily opened lunch box.

Peaches departs after opening up Allison like an electric can opener. We pull the remains of the mechanical shark back on deck. The thick, bullet-proof Lexan looks like a heap of plastic debris. Jean-Michel examines the shattered Lexan bars then looks in my direction. "Well, Steve, I guess this adds a certain dimension of excitement to your going into the plastic cylinder. Still feel comfortable about doing it?"

It almost surprises me when I automatically answer, "Yeah, I do."

Jean-Michel nods. "I agree. The plastic cage is safe."

Our decisions are based on a simple fact. Allison was not meant to withstand the attack of a great white shark. Her construction was designed for mobility, not strength. The latex skin, which gave Allison her realistic look, also provided a purchasing point for Peaches to anchor her massive teeth. My Lexan cage, however, was built to stand up to a serious shark attack. Though constructed of lighter plastic, the cage's cylindrical design greatly increases its strength.

Jean-Michel knows the plastic cage was soundly constructed; otherwise he never would have asked me to jump into it.

Unfortunately, sometimes "friends" encourage us to take foolish risks in the interest of proving ourselves. Often these childish dares are disguised as excuses for adventure. On the Cousteau expeditions, we often faced serious challenges, yet our adventures were always approached as calculated risks. Knowing the potential dangers, we would first take serious steps to minimize our exposure. Hazardous diving operations call for well thought-out plans and alternative courses of action for unexpected situations.

God has given each of us a dynamic body, that can be developed into a real adventure machine. He has also given us a highly developed brain for serious inquiry. To achieve our potential, and maybe even to ensure our own well-being, we should continuously exercise our ability to think for ourselves. We can never assume that someone else always has our best interests in mind, particularly when they are encouraging us to do something dangerous or potentially foolish.

> **To be blind is bad, but worse is
> it to have eyes and not to see.**
> **—Helen Keller**

As I write these thoughts, I again glance down at the newspaper on my desk. On the second page, there is an article about a silly young man. A cartoon on television had given him a novel idea. Last night, he laid down on the middle white line of a busy highway. Not surprisingly, an eighteen-wheeler truck accidentally ran him over. What is terribly important about this tragic story is that the victim, who suffered a painful and horrible death for his foolish stunt, was supposedly a normal teenager. Some of his friends had actually joined him in this crazy act. Apparently, thought they were being thrill seekers.

> The proverbs of Solomon: A wise son brings joy to his father,
> but a foolish son, grief to his mother. (Prov. 10:1)

Sometimes, what amounts to real courage is not going along with the group. A genuine leader cares about his or her friends. Leaders should encourage others to make positive choices. Often this means going against peer pressure, which can appear to be a powerful force to go up against. Going along with something, particularly when we know it is wrong, is always an act of weakness and stupidity. True challenges in life are found in standing up for what we know is right.

On the *Alcyone*, I am so safety conscious that the other divers often refer to me as *La Mère Poule* (the Mother Hen). It is a title I wear with pride and great satisfaction.

> **The task of the leader is to get his people from
> where they are to where they have not been.**
> **—Henry Kissinger**

Four

Not to forgive is to be imprisoned by the past.

—Anonymous

It is a blustery winter morning at Dangerous Reef. The wind is very cool as it blows across the quietly undulating ocean. I'm quite comfortable in my jeans and a warm sweat shirt as I lean against an idle shark cage on the *Alcyone's* stern. In my hand is a steaming cup of hot chocolate, which tastes rather funny. The sweet flavor is being tainted by a pungent reek of rotting fish floating in the air. It is wafting up from a rusty bait bucket a few feet away. There is nothing I can do about the foul odor; it permeates the whole ship. The horrible smell is necessary for attracting great white sharks. The stink of decaying fish is a delicious bouquet to sharks. Using the wind and tide, we are spreading an odor-corridor miles long. Any shark that stumbles into that corridor will eagerly follow the tempting stench to its source.

Peering hopefully over the side, I look to see if we have any morning visitors; that's when I see a dark shape rising rapidly to the surface just a few feet away. My heart leaps in anticipation as the creature surfaces and barks at me. *Rats*, I think to myself. Hoping for a shark, I instead look at a large pair of inquisitive eyes peering in a friendly way from the choppy water. The fur seal pup lifts its whiskered muzzle into the air and sniffs loudly.

Apparently, fur seals also find the aroma of rotting fish enticing. Reaching into the disgusting bait bucket, I carefully lift out a decomposing mackerel. The slimy fish feels squishy in my hand as I quickly flip it toward the fur seal, who swims

31

forward eagerly. Absent-mindedly lifting the steaming cocoa for another sip, my nose is instantly overwhelmed by the close-up smell of decomposing fish slime clinging to my hand. The horrible odor corrupts the chocolate flavor into something that could have risen from the bottom of a garbage can.

Lowering the cup, I notice the fur seal pup behaving strangely. It stops short of the fish and peers straight down into the water, then it flees in alarm toward Dangerous Reef.

Beneath the floating mackerel, I see a dark shadow torpe-doing upwards. An eighteen-foot-long great white shark lunges out of the water. Its gapping maw swallows the fish as white teeth glistening in the morning light clash loudly together. I momentarily see a lifeless orb staring at me, then the massive tail throws a broad slash of foaming white water. Quickly jumping back, I'm too late. The ice-cold salt water splashes across the stern, drenching my sweats and jeans.

Rushing for the bridge door, I throw it open and eagerly ring the ship's bell, while shouting, "Shark! Shark! All hands on deck."

Below deck there is instant pandemonium as the crew spills from staterooms. Some of them are still pulling on clothes; a few are carrying cameras as they run up the narrow corridor. At the lead is Bob Talbot, who is world famous for his creative photographs of whales and dolphins. Passing me, he notices that I am soaked head to foot. I can tell he is powerfully curious about why I am wet, but then the great white surfaces and begins vigorously biting the *Alcyone's* aluminum hull. The shark is in a feeding frenzy and looking for the food source leaking blood into the water. Since the blood is coming from the metal ship, it fits shark logic to bite it.

Bob runs past me and jumps down on the swim step. The small platform is only eight inches above the water and just several feet from the ship-chewing shark. Bob likes close-up photography. The shark helps by crashing mouth-first into the side of the swim step.

Soon the aggressive shark is joined by several toothy, equally aggressive friends. Bob and the rest of us couldn't be happier.

There are now four people crowding the small platform. Capkin attaches a line to a bait fish and uses it to lure the sharks directly to the swim step. Bob is leaning outward with a wide-angle lens shooting a seventeen-foot-long great white as it lunges for the bait fish. Missing, the shark slams back into the water, then it quickly dives beneath the swim step, passing directly under Bob's feet. It is a very exciting moment—then, without warning, it becomes terrifying.

Bob suddenly loses his balance. I see him falling helplessly into the water, his arms waving in panic. Incredibly, he lands right on the back of the great white shark. He bounces off the tall dorsal fin and slides into the water, where he is struck by the shark's tail. The superpredator, not expecting a 150-pound man to drop onto its back, bolts in surprise. A great white shark can turn around in its own length—and Bob is still thrashing in the water. Anxious hands quickly reach down to help, but he is slipping beneath the ship. There are at least three great white sharks off the stern, so we have to get him out fast. Finally, Bob reaches the surface, gasping and waving his hands frantically. Shockingly, one of those hands is still clutching his camera. Capkin and Therry grab hold of him and lift so hard that Bob all but flies out of the water, literally landing upright on his feet.

Bob is in a state of shock. He looks at his soaking wet camera, then peers over the side at a passing great white in pursuit of another shark.

"That was a really close call," offers Therry.

"How did you fall in?" asks Capkin.

"I don't know." Bob looks confused. "I guess I just fell."

Close to where they are standing, a large bait fish dangles three feet above the water's surface from our crane to encourage the great whites to lunge out of the water. Abruptly, one does. It is the same shark that Bob fell on only moments ago. Its monstrous jaws rip the forty-pound tuna in half in a single body-mangling bite, then the shark falls back into the water and disappears in a gigantic splash. The shark-generated wave splashes the already soaked divers on the swim step.

Bob stares slack-jawed at the mangled half of the tuna still dangling from the crane. "How did I fall in?" he asks no one in particular. Carrying his ruined camera, Bob goes below deck to change, leaving me with a very real dilemma.

Apparently, I am the only one who really saw what happened. Actually, someone else knows too, but so far he isn't prepared to talk about it.

When Bob was leaning over the water shooting pictures of the great white shark just beneath his feet, I was twelve feet away preparing to shoot a picture of him. I thought it would be a great action shot, so I focused a hundred millimeter lens on the crowded swim step. I clearly saw the fourth person on that platform. He was behind the others, shooting with a video camera. He had one eye open to look through the video view finder and the other eye closed to eliminate visual distractions. When the shark swam under the swim step, he had taken a step forward for a better view. With the one eye closed, he blindly placed his free hand out to steady himself. His hand landed on Bob's shoulder, accidentally shoving him into the water.

He is now standing in the background of the rest of the activity. I know I am going to have to confront him. Bob needs to know that it wasn't his own fault. As a wildlife photographer, he has a very dangerous job. He must have complete confidence in his physical abilities or his future performance might suffer. I wait until the other man is alone.

"I saw that it was an accident," I offer.

"Yeah, he just fell in," the other man says lamely.

I shake my head, saying, "No, you did it accidentally when you were trying to keep your own balance."

"No way!" the man argues.

"Look, you didn't do it on purpose. Bob will understand that," I reply, putting a hand on his shoulder. "But you've got to tell him."

The man shakes off my hand. "I didn't do it," he rages, then he storms below, slamming the metal door.

Looking unhappily at the closed door, I now have an even bigger dilemma. This is turning into an ugly situation and there is only one solution.

> **The truth doesn't hurt unless it ought to.**
> —B.C. Forbes

In life, sometimes people argue for not telling the truth when it might hurt themselves or another person. To varying degrees, these falsehoods are referred to as "white lies." We lie to someone supposedly to protect them or ourselves, but from what? The truth? Honesty is always the best solution. Lies inevitably wind up hurting everyone involved.

Going below, I find Bob in his cabin and quietly tell him what really happened. Though he is rightfully angry that the man didn't take responsibility for his actions, Bob also realizes it really was just an unfortunate accident. But, more importantly, Bob realizes it wasn't his own fault.

Half an hour later he is again standing on the swim step taking extreme close-up pictures of sharks. Capkin and Therry are there to help lure in the great whites, but no one is standing behind Bob, something I see Bob confirming for himself with regular glances over his shoulder.

I see the man I confronted standing alone by the bridge. He is looking rather sheepish and unsettled. Right now, the open knowledge of his mistake is making him uncomfortable, but it is a feeling that will pass, probably in just a day or two. However, had he kept the lie, it would have burdened him far into the future—maybe even for the rest of his life. One of life's simple lessons that sometimes seems so hard to learn is that lies enslave us, while the truth sets us free.

Kings take pleasure in honest lips; they value a man who speaks the truth. (Prov. 16:13)

Five

Jesus answered, "I am the way and the truth and the life. No one comes to the Father except through me."

—John 14:6

It is late in the night. Lying on my bunk, I'm still thinking about the negative impact of not being completely honest, particularly to ourselves. Truth is one of our greatest personal strengths. From it we draw courage to stand up for what we know is right and good. To compromise truth is to weaken the foundation of our spirit and character. I learned this lesson the hard way, by making a very big mistake.

> **Life sometimes gives you the test before you've had a chance to study the lesson.**
> **—Anonymous**

Surprisingly, the day my life shifted in a truly negative way began on a beautiful morning in a tropical paradise.

I am with three brand-new friends, and we are on a surf safari. The Volkswagen bus is just passing out of a light rain on the north shore of Oahu in Hawaii. Looking out the VW's window, I see the morning sun painting a spectacular rainbow against towering, dark volcanic mountains. About us, the lush sugarcane fields stretch for miles. The trade winds are playing amongst the sugarcane, causing the grassy fields to ripple like an undulating green sea.

Inside the Volkswagen bus, we are carrying a full load. The cramped interior is overwhelmed with four surfers, breakfast debris from a Taco Bell, an assortment of towels (in various states of cleanliness), three surfboards (there are four more on

top), and a very excited Great Dane. Currently, the dog (my abnormally large Dane) has his face jammed ear-deep into an empty, salsa-stained burrito bag. For some reason, Puu Bear really likes hot sauce. The spicier it is, the more he likes to wolf it down, though he sometimes whines with his tail wagging at turbo speed.

I get his attention with a tortilla chip. "Want this, boy?"

He sniffs, licks, and chomps in what appears to be a single motion. I wipe a bit of dog drool off my hand onto Sam's towel, while he stares intently out the front windshield. Driving requires Sam's full attention. With him behind the wheel, driving is always a challenging experience. All of us are alert to warn him of any possible misadventures.

He takes a corner too fast, putting a serious tilt on the VW bus. Everyone inside leans hard right, particularly Puu Bear, who is actually attempting to get closer to Mark's soft taco.

"Get off me, you big lug," complains Mark. He tries to push the oversized dog away, mistakenly allowing the hand with the taco to come within muzzle range. Chomp!

"Hey!" Mark is appalled. "Your clod dog just ate my taco." Then staring at his not-completely-empty hand, he asks, "Is that drool? Oh, wow. I just got dog-slimed."

I pass him Sam's towel.

As the Volkswagen tops a rise between two sprawling sugarcane fields, we get our first view of the coastline. There is a major swell pounding the north shore. Everyone leans forward for a better view, including Puu Bear, who is actually checking out the front seat for any more unguarded goodies.

"Looks big!" Sam states the obvious while downshifting into third, which causes a shutter that vibrates the length of the van. The front tires have been out of alignment ever since he tried taking the VW bus up a skateboard ramp.

"Really big," I offer from the back seat.

"Could be scary, but fun," Mark says hopefully.

"Woof," Puu Bear joins our enthusiasm. None of us, however, know what he is excited about.

"I think your dog is eating something," Mark says, suspiciously leaning forward to check the front seat.

"Nothing up here to eat," replies Sam. "Keno already wasted all our groceries."

Keno, a large Hawaiian sitting in the passenger seat, pretends to be offended then belches contentedly and shakes taco crumbs from his T-shirt.

Mark attempts to take a closer look inside Puu Bear's crocodile mouth, which proves to be a mistake when the big dog abruptly chokes and coughs. A heavy, moist cloud of white bits impacts Mark's face from just inches away. "Yuck," he complains loudly, then quickly scrubs at his face with Sam's towel.

I examine one of the white bits, instantly solving the mystery. "It's Keno's surfboard wax."

"Oh, man!" Now, Keno is upset. "That was a brand-new bar."

"Smells like coconuts. No wonder Puu Bear ate it," I answer. Puu loves cracking coconuts with his massive jaws. I rub Puu Bear's ears, then use Sam's towel to wipe the rest of the wax and drool debris off his broad muzzle and flick the towel into the back of the VW.

Fifteen minutes later we arrive at Lannikia Beach Park and everyone unloads into the parking lot. The surf is bigger than our expectations. We stare in awkward silence. None of us wants to admit that the surf looks really scary. The waves are almost two stories tall and crash down with a sound like rolling thunder.

"I think I'm gonna need a bigger board," offers Sam.

"What do you think?" I ask Keno. "Is it too big?" As a new surfer, I am having very real reservations about paddling out into what looks to be dangerous conditions.

"Aah, you guys just need some courage," answers the big Hawaiian. He pulls a marijuana cigarette out of his shirt pocket, lights up, and passes it to Sam. As the joint heads in my direction, I have plenty of time to think if I should really do this.

I first tried marijuana in Vietnam during the war. I did not like how it clouded my mind and made a positive decision to avoid other servicemen who used drugs. Three years later, I was transferred to EODMUONE (Explosive Ordnance Disposal

Mobile Unit One), a frogman bomb disposal command in Hawaii. Being a water-oriented person living on an island paradise, I naturally took up the sport of surfing; however, with the sport came new friends, some of whom were regular marijuana users. Keno and Mark were such friends.

Sam, who only recently tried marijuana for the first time, chokes on the harsh smoke and all but doubles over in a sudden coughing spasm. A cloud of smoke erupts from his mouth and nose as his eyes begin to water. "Stuff burns," he complains, then offers the joint to me.

From what I have just seen, I know this is not a good idea.

"Hurry up," Mark complains. "The roach is gonna go out, man."

Everyone is staring at me and waiting. Surfing is such a fun new adventure, and I want these guys to like me.

Awkwardly, I grasp the joint, which doesn't look appetizing at all. The lit end of the cigarette is charred and emitting an acrid smoke; the other end is brown and wet with saliva from two other people. As I hesitate, Sam gasps loudly and coughs again.

"Do it, dude," says Keno as he strikes a match, touching the flame to the end of the blackened joint.

Reluctantly, I raise the cigarette and, trying not to touch my lips, take a slight pull. Instantly, the acrid smoke burns my throat and lungs. I immediately blow the harsh fumes back out as Mark eagerly snatches the joint from my hand and takes a deep pull.

The joint passes from hand to hand, then back to me. It is now barely half-an-inch in length. My reaction is to throw it away. Keno stops me by saying, "Don't waste it, dude." The Hawaiian has his hand on mine. "Take another drag, only this time hold the smoke in."

I'm already feeling light-headed. The smoke scorches my throat again, then the flame abruptly runs down the paper as a smoking ember flies burning into my mouth.

"Aah!" I shout, pawing at my singed lips.

"What a lightweight," laughs Keno, knuckling me in the chest.

While the other guys begin waxing up their surfboards, I chain Puu Bear to a coconut tree. After making sure there is plenty of slack in the chain (so Puu can't wrap it up), I become aware of how strange I am feeling. It is almost as if my body and I are no longer connected. I find the odd feeling very unsettling. Placing a bucket of water out for Puu, I rush to join my friends.

Mark and Keno are already running out into the water, so I quickly grab my board.

"Better hurry," urges Sam. He wipes his hand on his towel, then sniffs suspiciously at his hands. "Wow!" he says, wrinkling his nose. "I hope that wasn't something I ate."

"I'm feeling really funny," I confide while attaching the surfboard leash to my leg.

Sam nods his head knowingly. "Why do you think they call it dope?"

At the water's edge, I pause to stare again at the heavy surf. There is a lot of white water and strong, conflicting onshore currents.

"Well, here goes nothing," shouts Sam, launching himself into the water. I hesitate then follow, still feeling very weird and clumsy in my movements.

Sam dunks his board under the first oncoming wave, then swims safely out the back side. Because of my muddled condition, I have forgotten to wax-up my surfboard. Without the traction of the rough wax coating, the wave instantly washes me off the slick board. By the time I recover and begin paddling out again, the other guys are fifty yards ahead of me.

Alone, I paddle hard to catch my friends. The surf is breaking with a heavy whomping sound like rolling thunder. It looks even bigger out here, particularly from the flat perspective of laying on a surfboard. As I get farther out, the surf gets bigger and scarier.

In my pot-fogged brain, alarms are going off. I want to turn around and retreat to the beach. Worrying what my friends may think, I reluctantly continue paddling out. Peer pressure is a powerful force.

Before me, an oncoming wave breaks with a thunderous sound as it cascades into a wall of angry white water. Thrashing my way into the oncoming wall of water, I am again flushed from my board. I surface, choking and spitting saltwater, to see my friends paddling frantically up the face of a two-story wave. Then, I see the cause for their haste.

Farther out, a freak wave is heading for the beach. It is a giant wave towering twenty feet into the air. Momentarily, I lose sight of the monstrous wave as I begin paddling wildly up the face of the next wave of the set. My heart races with exertion. Reaching the top, I plunge down the backside. A spray of saltwater temporarily clouds my vision. Furiously, I paddle, trying to beat the oncoming avalanche of water before it breaks; already the top curl is beginning to pitch. My friends reach the top and disappear over the back. The giant wave is pulling the water before it toward itself, causing it to build and grow even larger. Aided by the oncoming current, I sprint up the turbulent, nearly vertical face. The thick lip throws outward as I struggle to fight my way up and over the top. I feel the gigantic wave pitching forward, pulling the surrounding water and its small human cargo irresistibly backward. I fight the pull, paddling with all my might. At the last instant, I barely break free. Out of breath and exhausted, I slide down the back side of the breaker, and that's when I see the next wave.

The first two waves are no more than doormats for what is coming. It is known as a clean-up wave; it wipes everything away that is before it. The wave is only a few feet taller than the last one, but it is much thicker and already breaking. I watch a wall of white water more than two stories tall swallow my friends. Taking a deep breath, I push my board away and frantically dive for the bottom.

One of the many negative characteristics of marijuana smoking is that the user's awareness and perception suffer. Having already forgotten to wax up my surfboard, I now forget to remove the surfboard leash from my leg. The surfboard floating on the surface keeps me from getting very deep. I turn to free my leg, just as the wall of water crashes into me. It is like being slugged with a hydraulic sledgehammer. The sharp impact pounds the air from my lungs. I feel the surfboard leash go taut, then it begins pulling me, spinning me wildly in its wake, like an out-of-control kite in a gale. Soberly, I realize I might be about to die. Instantly, I wish with all my might that I hadn't gotten stoned. My tortured lungs carry the burden of the damaging smoke. I cannot hold my breath much longer as I am pulled violently backwards through the raging water. Wondering if my life is about to end, the thought that flashes through my mind is, Who will unchain Puu Bear?

Suddenly, the rubber surfboard leash breaks, slowing my terrifying horizontal journey. Struggling with all my might, I barely make it to the surface. Frantically, I take two deep breaths before being hit by another wave. I must have taken four or five trips on the underwater subway that morning.

Finally, totally exhausted, the four of us made it back to the beach, minus a broken surfboard. I thought it the most foolish day of my life—but actually it was just the beginning of a series of stupid mistakes.

The most important thing I remember about that day is not the size of the surf. Actually, I would encounter big surf on many other occasions. No, that is the day when I stood on the threshold of two possible futures—and made a really bad choice. Because of peer pressure and my own foolishness, I would soon become a regular marijuana user. I didn't realize it then, but I was about to become a hostage to marijuana. Later, I would sacrifice positive times with my friends and other fun opportunities just to get stoned. Eventually, that first bad marijuana choice would lead to my incarceration for three years in a federal prison.*

In the darkness of the wind ship's stateroom, I lie on my bunk and think about choices. People seldom choose to do something wrong by themselves. It is not our enemies who encourage us to do drugs. Unfortunately, it is always a friend—

---

*Author's note: The details of my self-inflicted incarceration associated with marijuana use and illegal drug transportation are explained in my book *Journey into Darkness* by Huntington House Publishers (Lafayette, La., 1992).

or worse yet, a family member. Bad choices are one of the results of poor relationships. It is a progressive type of corruption that steals the happiness and self-worth of all concerned. A real friend encourages his or her peers to make positive, life-enhancing choices. Positive restraint is a graceful kind of strength.

> Buy the truth and do not sell it; get wisdom, discipline and understanding. (Prov. 23:23)

Six

Obstacles are what you see when you take your eyes off your goal.

—Anonymous

It is just before sunrise on another stormy winter day. I am standing at the stern of the *Alcyone*, staring at the stars and just finishing the 2:00 to 5:00 A.M. watch. The wind is howling across Dangerous Reef, causing the *Alcyone* to swing like a pendulum at her anchorage. I'm trying not to breathe through my nose because a horrible cargo of really pungent odors is riding the wind from Dangerous Reef. The tiny spit of rock is a sea bird rookery and fur seal whelping sanctuary. The reef smells worse than an overstuffed diaper pail.

I know there isn't a chance of launching the shark cages today, yet part of my watch requires that I continue the chum corridor drifting behind the wind ship. Scooping up a bucket of fish offal, tuna oil, and dried blood, I lean over the stern and pour it into the dark water. I'm trying to keep the awful stuff from splashing onto my pants, so I'm pouring it slowly. Apparently, this gives the great white shark all the time it needs to zero in on the source, because Amy erupts at my feet, biting viciously at the chum steam. Leaping wildly out of the way, I inadvertently spill fish offal onto my 501 jeans.

Desperate to change my pants, I instead wipe off the grosser chunks before rushing into the bridge to grab my camera. Quickly loading it with high-speed film, I dash back outside. I am tying a rotting mackerel to a piece of rope with a yellow balloon on it when Capkin arrives along with the sunrise.

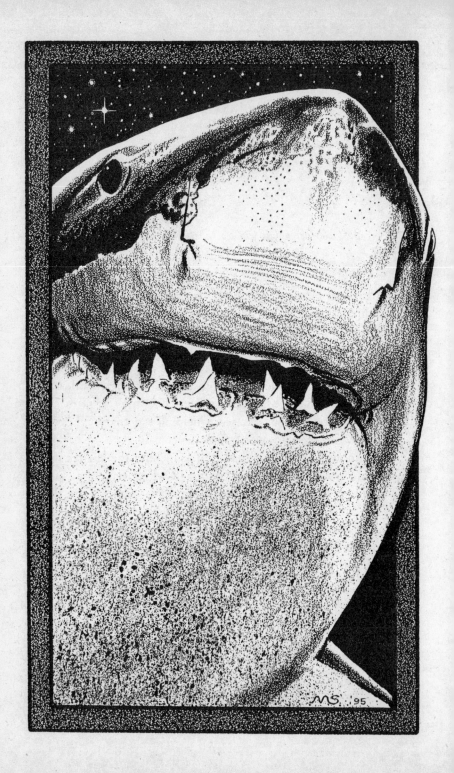

"Wow! That's some smell out here," Capkin states the obvious as he steps through the bridge door. He takes several very deep breaths through his nose then he snorts loudly.

"Don't tell me you like that foul odor?" I ask in surprise.

"Not at all," Capkin states cheerfully. "By overloading the nose all at once, I get use to it sooner. The smell practically goes away."

"Really?" I answer, hazarding several deeper breaths myself. I feel my nose wrinkling in protest. My legs are also not very happy with the slimy feeling of the chum-clinging jeans.

"Why are you tying that decaying fish to a balloon? Making a party favor for someone?" Capkin's good mood is a direct result of his having just left the breakfast table.

"It's an experiment," I grin in a friendly way, mostly because I'm looking for a second set of hands. "Want to help?"

"Sure, just as long as I don't have to touch your stinky fish." Capkin is the most enthusiastic person I know, which also explains why he usually has more fun than anyone else in the crew.

I excitedly tell him that I want to re-create the poster from the movie *Jaws*. The *Jaws* poster is actually a painting, depicting a great white shark leaping right at you with its massive mouth wide open—only I'm intent on doing it with a real shark. Amy's morning leap has given me the unique idea of dangling a fish from the wind ship's crane, which is why I need Capkin's help.

I thread the rope through the tip of the crane then lower the fish into the water. The floating yellow balloon will keep the fish near the surface. When the great white lunges for the bait, Capkin must quickly pull the fish straight up. To get the fish, Amy is going to have to leap for it.

"I like it," says Capkin, enthusiastically taking hold of the rope. "Where will you stand to take the picture?"

"The swim step," I answer, jumping down onto the tiny platform, which is just eight inches above the water.

"This should be real interesting," Capkin deadpans. "What happens if the leaping shark lands on the swim step?"

"I imagine I'll get off it rather rapidly," I respond while wondering if this is really a bright idea.

While the fish is dangling in the water under the yellow balloon, I try taking several more deep breaths through my nose, but each time the foul stench remains just as intensely horrible. "Are you sure this breathing deeply through the nose reduces the smell's impact?" I ask in despair.

"No," Capkin replies cheerfully. "I just wanted to see if you would be stupid enough to try it."

I'm about to say something in reply, but the great white shark erupts from the water at my feet, ending our conversation. Amy is the bad-tempered shark with the serious attitude problem. She lunges for the dead fish, which completely surprises her by flying straight-up out of the water. The astonished shark tries to pursue but, lacking momentum, falls back into the water instead. Amy makes five more unsuccessful lunges for the fish before her bad disposition sends the now thoroughly angry shark into a biting frenzy. Shark scientists refer to this activity as display behavior. Amy is swimming in circles furiously biting empty water repeatedly.

"Looks like Amy is getting a mite stirred-up." Capkin tugs lightly on the line, making the bait fish wiggle invitingly.

The enraged shark circles the floating balloon with its dancing fish baggage then reverses direction and rapidly swims straight down. "Uh oh," I caution Capkin. "I think this might be it. She's going deep."

Seconds later, I see the dark shape of the shark torpedoing vertically upward like a ballistic missile. As Capkin jerks the fish rapidly upwards, the three-thousand-pound shark explodes from the water, its massive mouth wide open, giant teeth flashing in the sunlight. Her tail drives furiously, propelling her a full six feet above the shark-thrashed water. Quickly, leaning outward with my camera, I shoot a full-frame picture of the fierce predator from only three feet away. Seeing the enraged shark filling the view finder, I release the shutter, knowing that it is the picture I am hoping for. I'm about to shout with glee, when the balloon and bait fish lands with a solid plop onto the swim step. Caught up in all the excitement, Capkin has accidentally let go of the rope.

Uh oh, I think to myself. The shark, still in aerial pursuit, looks in my direction but fortunately falls short. She slams back into the water right next to the tiny platform. The shark bellywhomper instantly flushes me head-to-toe with freezing saltwater. For a moment I'm completely stunned, which sends Capkin into a fit of laughter.

I look at him and grin, then abruptly I hear a loud grinding sound on the swim platform to my rear. Quickly spinning around, I see the shark right behind me. Amy is angrily chewing on the aluminum swim step. The teeth, gashing repeatedly on metal, are only a foot from my bare toes. Instinctively, I leap backwards and land on the inflated balloon. The sharp sound of the bursting balloon startles me. I almost leap again but suddenly remember the shark chomping away at the swim step.

"Hurry, get a picture," shouts Capkin.

I had forgotten about the camera in my hand. I quickly raise it and push the shutter release, but nothing happens. The shark attacks the swim step a final time, leaving foot-long scrapes in the white paint, then it disappears beneath the stern with an angry flick of its tail.

I take a long breath to slow my beating heart, no longer aware of the foul scent in the air. Excitement always captures the whole mind's attention. Next, I take a closer look at the camera. It is soaking wet.

"That's the second camera you've flooded this year," says Jean-Michel gravely as he steps out of the *Alcyone's* bridge. I soaked another camera on the previous expedition when I got too close to a breaching humpback whale.

"I can fix the camera, and the film inside is fine," I answer happily. "Just wait until you see this shot."

Jean-Michel nudges Capkin, "Do you see what is oozing up from his feet?"

Glancing down, I see that I am standing barefoot on the rotting mackerel. Some of the squashed fish is grossly seeping up between my toes.

"Don't you have anything better to do than play with the bait?" complains Jean-Michel.

Thoroughly washing my jeans and feet later does not eliminate the smell of decaying fish. It is the reason why the rest of the crew bands me from eating dinner in the salon.

Sitting alone in the captain's chair on the bridge with a large salad propped between my knees, I think about real life choices. Most of us want adventure and challenge in our lives, yet few people actually take the time and effort to do something constructive about it.

> Creative man lives many lives; some men are so dull they do not live even once.
> —Dagobert D. Runes

There are two very real conditions to discovering challenge and adventure in life. They both require an active lifestyle and an inquisitive mind. Captain Cousteau once said, "The primary motivator in my life is curiosity." The world, right outside each of our front doors, is full of wonder, mystery, and potential adventure. The challenge is merely to step outside and look for the unexpected, then to get involved with it.

My afternoon adventure with Amy wouldn't have happened had I not been actively looking for a new way to shoot dramatic pictures of great white sharks. Instead of being inquisitive, I could have just sat on the stern and done nothing— and, of course, nothing would have been my appropriate reward. Boredom is self-inflicted.

> Activity is the only medicine I take. It's very efficient.
> —Captain Jacques-Yves Cousteau

Seven

And so we know and rely on the love God has for us. God is love. Whoever lives in love lives in God, and God in him.
—1 John 4:16

I'm still on the bridge, just finishing repairs on the camera. Looking out the bridge's windows, I see it is going to be a truly fabulous night. Beyond the wind ship's bow, the blazing orb of the setting sun leisurely falls from a cloud-studded sky. The fading daystar washes a bank of clouds near the horizon with bright red light as it slowly slips behind Dangerous Reef. At the reef's highest point, a small group of fur seal pups are momentarily silhouetted in brilliant red light. They are playing "king of the rock." I can hear their happy barks above the rhythmic sound of the surf.

Glancing at the top of the thirty-foot turbo sail, I see the wind indicator barely registering a soft breeze blowing from the reef. It means that (other than me) there will be no unusual smells tonight. In about twenty minutes, a full moon will be rising out of the east, and I am making plans to liven up the evening. All I need is a little help.

Right on cue, an unsuspecting Capkin steps through the door. Raising a finger to his lips for secrecy, he quietly opens a floor hatch and drops into the reefer below. Like most ships at sea, the *Alcyone* has to carry a large supply of fresh fruits, vegetables, and dairy products. The reefer beneath the bridge is huge and stocked full of good things to eat. Therefore, it isn't surprising that the reefer happens to be one of Capkin's favorite places. Bruno, the chef, would have a fit if he knew that Capkin was raiding the grocery locker.

"Hey, Capkin," I whisper. "Want to help me with another experiment?"

Capkin's head momentarily appears through the hatch. "When?" he mumbles, taking a big bite out of a large red apple.

"In about fifteen minutes," I reply.

"Ah, Steve," Capkin frowns around his apple. "The guys are going to watch a really good video in the salon."

"Capkin, I'm ashamed of you," I tease. "Are you going to sit in front of a boob tube, when there's adventure happening outside?"

"What kind of adventure?" Capkin asks suspiciously.

"Kind of like what we did this afternoon," I say, loading a fresh roll of film into the camera.

"Are you nuts?" Capkin mumbles, having forgotten about the apple in his face. "It's gonna be dark in fifteen minutes."

"I know," I answer holding up a flash attachment for the camera.

"How are we going to see the shark coming?" He remembers the apple and takes a bite.

"Lunar light," I grin. "The moon will be rising in fifteen minutes, and it will make a great background for the shark."

"OK, I'm in." Capkin's head disappears back down the hatch.

Looking down inside the reefer, I see Capkin busily filling his pockets with a wedge of cheese, two handfuls of nuts, and a banana. Reaching under a wooden crate, he pulls out Bruno's secret stash of cooking chocolate. He breaks off a thick piece, which immediately goes into his mouth.

I start to walk away.

"Where are you going?" Capkin asks softly.

"In pursuit of a decaying mackerel," I answer, closing the bridge door behind me.

Outside, I pause to appreciate the incredible beauty of the ocean in twilight. I watch the last red glow of the sunset fading behind Dangerous Reef. For a few seconds, there is a lingering shadow of crimson playing on the dark, rippling water, then the rapid onset of nightfall brings forth a vast parade of stars glistening in the heavens. In the east, there is a dim glow of pale light hugging the horizon in anticipation of the moonrise.

Happily, I don a pair of Capkin's wet suit gloves and muck about in the fish bucket for a mackerel. Tying it to the rope still hanging from the crane, I decide not to add a balloon after what happened last time.

Capkin arrives with his pockets bulging, just in time to take his end of the rope. Stepping down onto the swim step, I know I won't have a long wait. Half an hour earlier, I saw four large sharks aggressively circling the *Alcyone's* stern.

Peering into the dark water, I see a dark shape silently sliding beneath the wind ship's stern. I hear a sudden splash in the shadowed darkness beyond our stern light then a rapid swishing of water, like something is being chased. Getting the camera ready, I briefly wonder if the sharks are being more active because of the full moon.

Capkin echoes my thoughts. "Looks like the buggers like to play when the moon is full." Two great whites, one in pursuit of the other, pass the *Alcyone's* stern like torpedoes. I move to the back of the swim step just to be a little bit farther from the dark water. Inside my head, my subconscious plays with dark images of flashing teeth.

"OK, Capkin, lower the fish," I say nervously.

The mackerel barely hits the water before a great white instantly steals it.

"Well, that was fun," announces Capkin. "Can I go watch my movie now?"

I lift the shredded end of the rope. "I need another fish."

In the next half hour, we lose six fish. All we get to see are their slick backs shimmering in the moonlight as they depart with my fish. I have long since abandoned using Capkin's wet suit gloves. Plunging my bare hands elbow-deep into the bait bucket, I lift out a squishy fish and tie it brutally to the rope.

"OK, last try," I assure Capkin, who is beginning to get impatient.

"By the way, you know those aren't my gloves, don't you?" snickers Capkin.

I glance down at the thoroughly slimed gloves, "They're not?"

"No, they're Jean-Michel's," giggles Capkin. "I put them by the bait bucket, figuring you'd trap yourself."

Suddenly, I see a disturbance in the moonlight dancing on the black water. Aiming my camera, I warn Capkin, "Get ready, here it comes!"

The shark actually seems to slow as it erupts from the water. It comes up completely vertical, so slowly that there is no threat of it reaching me. It misses the fish, giving me a great opportunity. I lean forward aiming the camera almost into its mouth and release the shutter. The camera's strobe flashes brightly as I get the first-ever picture of a great white shark—belching!

Caught in the instantaneous flash of light, I see that a great white belch is a visible affair. There isn't a chance of my getting out of the way. It is coming straight at me in a thick misty cloud. It impacts my face. Instantly, I can tell there are moist chunks mixed in with the shark saliva. I turn to look at Capkin; one of my eyes is glued shut with slimy shark slobber.

"Yuck!" announces Capkin. "The shark barfed on you."

An hour later, after thoroughly washing Jean-Michel's gloves—and my face—I lay out my Coleman sleeping bag on the wind ship's main deck. I've decided to sleep outside, particularly since the captain won't let me into our cabin. The moist pieces in the shark belch were, of course, ground putrefying mackerel. Though I scrubbed and scrubbed, I still carry the lingering bouquet of fish rot and shark barf. The slight odor coming from Dangerous Reef no longer bothers me at all.

Climbing into the sleeping bag, I enjoy the comfortable feeling of the soft flannel. It stirs up boyhood memories and, for a moment, I think back to that young person and his wild hopes and aspirations. How surprised he would be if he could see me now.

> To accomplish great things, we must not only act, but also dream; not only plan, but also believe.
> —Anatole France

I was just a typical kid. I got average grades in school and didn't excel at any one sport. I wasn't particularly popular, but had a close circle of a few good friends. I didn't belong to any school clubs, because I usually worked after school mowing lawns, picking weeds, and washing cars. I needed the money because my father divorced our family just when I hit my teens. My dad always seemed uncomfortable around my brother and me. He had one golden rule for us boys. I remember it well because he said it all the time: "Go to your room and play quietly or go outside."

Despite himself, I know my father loved his children. He just didn't know how to show it. I recently read a survey that claims fathers, on the national average, are only spending approximately seven and a half minutes a week of quality time with their sons.

I think it must be awfully tough for many young people growing up in today's busy society. We may wonder where we fit in, or even if anyone really cares. In the middle of all this, we must daily make important choices. Unfortunately, some young people just give up. They drop out of school, leave their families, and flee into the unknown. It's scary to attempt to face life in a mostly uncaring world alone. Each and every day, over thirteen hundred teen-agers attempt suicide in America.

The most important thing I can say about all of this is that Christ loves us no matter who we are or what we've done. He is a beacon of hope and of goodness. God's houses on earth are safe refuges of love and care. His sanctuaries are in every city and town across North and South America. When we are lost, He is always looking for us with open arms. We only have to knock at His door.

> Learn to do right! Seek justice, encourage the oppressed. Defend the cause of the fatherless, plead the case of the widow. (Isa. 1:17)

Eight

By wisdom a house is built, and through understanding it is established; through knowledge its rooms are filled with rare and beautiful treasures.

—Proverbs 24:3-4

I arrive early at the airport with a large sunflower. I am also wearing a radiant smile. It is the second thing people notice, right after the big sunflower. I stand at the arrival gate in eager anticipation. Finally, the plane arrives and people are soon walking down the ramp. As Cindy, my girlfriend, leaves the plane she sees the flower (towering above the heads of the waiting crowd) and instantly she knows I am close by.

A moment later Cindy is in my arms. "Welcome to Hawaii," I grin, handing her the gargantuan blossom.

"According to Hawaiian tradition you are supposed to meet me with a flower lei." Cindy is most happy when she is giving me a hard time.

"But this is such a nice sunflower," I say in the flower's defense. "It really wanted to come to the airport, and it is very pleased that you are here."

This is my third date with Cindy. I have asked her to join our Cousteau expedition in Maui, Hawaii, where we are diving with humpback whales. An hour later, she and I are walking down a floating pier in the Lahaina yacht harbor. It is early morning and our boat will soon be getting underway.

For this expedition, I have chartered a thirty-two-foot, twin-screwed cabin cruiser named *Sea Otter*. This is a very fast boat. Jean-Michel Cousteau and Michel DeLoire, our cinematographer, are on deck prepping an underwater cinema camera.

Cindy is beginning to get nervous about joining the Cousteau expedition. The only member of the team she knows is Jean-Michel Cousteau. "Steve," she takes my arm, "I really want to be a part of the team, so don't hesitate to put me to work. I can cook, wash dishes, help with the diving gear—anything."

"I already have a job for you," I smile mischievously.

"Chief deck scrubber?" Cindy grins, squeezing my arm.

"No," I deadpan. "Actually, I thought you might drive the boat."

"What?" Cindy sputters.

As a student missionary in the South Pacific, Cindy spent a lot of time operating small craft. She also worked a summer job in a marina, so I know she is well qualified for the assignment.

"Would you rather wash the dishes?" I ask playfully.

"Treat your skipper with more respect or I'll have you scrubbing the deck, sailor," Cindy replies, punching me lightly in the chest to reinforce her statement. I like being punched by Cindy; it means she is in a playful mood.

"Yes ma'am, Captain Bligh," I answer. As always, I'm surprised at how quickly Cindy adapts to new situations.

Though I am already carrying her heavy dive bag, she abruptly slings her other bag into my free hand. "Quick, take this."

"Why?" I ask.

Cindy grins, "Because, silly, I need both of my hands for hugging Jean-Michel Cousteau."

For the next week, Cindy's main job is to keep the charter boat in the general vicinity of our dive operations as a support vessel. From it, we reload the cameras, charge our scuba tanks, and launch the rubber Zodiacs for approaching the whales. Unfortunately, this means that Cindy is always a good distance from the main whale activity—that is, until that one special day.

It is a blustery, stormy morning toward the end of the expedition. The gusting wind is whipping the surface into frothy white caps. The Zodiacs are in close attendance with a fast-moving pod of fifteen whales when the humpbacks make an abrupt turn directly toward our support vessel. Jean-Michel Cousteau, who is operating the outboard, quickly grabs a walkie-talkie.

"Cindy, this is Jean-Michel," he calls urgently.

"Cindy here," comes the rapid reply.

"Shut down your engines. The whales are heading straight for you." Jean-Michel turns our Zodiac and goes in rapid pursuit.

"Roger, going dead in the water," Cindy answers, then hoots loudly. Hearing her eager enthusiasm, I look in the distance to see Cindy prancing down from the flying bridge for a close-up view of the oncoming humpbacks. The whale pod we are following consists of a single female and the rest are all large males. It is the end of the breeding season and the cow is running from fourteen hefty admirers, each of whom weighs up to twenty-five tons. She is trying to flee, but the only apparent shelter is Cindy's boat.

On board the *Sea Otter*, Cindy has no idea why fifteen whales are heading in her direction. She is just ecstatic to be in their path, not realizing that her little boat is actually their destination. The whales, which are some of the largest creatures on earth, are coming at full speed. Cindy couldn't be happier as she sees the charging cow surface fifty feet away. The massive humpback is torpedoing straight for the small boat. When the approaching whales are only twenty feet away, the cow submerges, passing mere feet beneath the *Sea Otter's* keel. Cindy rushes to the other side, expecting to see the huge whale swimming away; instead, she gets the shock of her life.

The cow has gone from full speed to a dead stop, as she tries to hide by lying alongside the small cabin cruiser. The thirty-two-foot-long boat only shelters the front half of the massive whale. Cindy's shriek of surprise is drowned out completely by the boisterous arrival of the fourteen bulls. Some of them breech, lifting their twenty-five-ton bodies high out of the water, then slam back into the ocean with tremendous force. White water from whale-induced belly whompers explodes into the air. The strong trade winds send a cascade of falling water showering across the boat's deck, soaking Cindy—much to her delight.

The bulls fight amongst themselves, each trying to get next to the cow. They ram each other repeatedly, littering the water with small, floating pieces of whale skin from the enormous impacts. The mad excitement increases as several of the inflamed bulls swing their mammoth tails high into the air. For a heart-stopping moment, their giant flukes wave vigorously two stories above the water, doubling the height of the *Sea Otter*, then the tails slam down with tremendous force. The sharp impacts echo across the water like a row of cannons firing in rapid succession. Amazingly, with all this incredible sound, I can still hear Cindy's yelps of ecstatic excitement. The thirty-two-foot boat rocks wildly from side to side.

The cow, realizing that her sanctuary isn't so safe, abruptly makes a run for it. She submerges under the *Sea Otter* and flees with powerful strokes of her tail. The bulls charge in pursuit. Many of them pass under the *Sea Otter*. Currents from their wakes beat against the boat's hull sending it spinning first in one direction, then the other.

The whales are now heading toward the Zodiacs. Jean-Michel cuts the engine and yells, "Quick, everyone into the water!" Michel DeLoire is the first one to react as he snatches a mask and rolls over the side. Grabbing an underwater camera, I quickly slip in after him. Together, we take several rapid breaths, filling our lungs with air. The whales are but fifty yards away when we both dive beneath the stormy water.

Beneath the surface the water is deceptively calm, then we see the whales hurling at us. It is amazing to be in the path of animals the size of eighteen-wheeler trucks and Greyhound buses. The humpbacks are racing ten times faster than human swimming speed. It will be impossible for us to get out of their way. It is one of the risks of working with wild animals. Yet, even in their excitement, the whales are graceful swimmers. Long pectoral fins extend from their bodies like wings of a giant bird in flight. Incredibly, each of the racing whales slightly alters its course to keep from running over the two tiny creatures in its path.

The cow passes just beneath us. Michel DeLoire and I stop our descent as the rest of the whales begin rushing past us. For thirty long seconds we are in the midst of the vast pod. The mammoth bodies gliding by seem almost surrealistic because there is absolutely no sound. Two of the whales pass directly above us, their massive shadows momentarily blotting out the sunlight. Out of breath, we begin to ascend directly behind them, only I get caught in the strong surge of a whale wake that sends me momentarily spinning wildly out of control.

On the surface we both pant for air. Between gasps, the trade winds faintly bring me the sound of Cindy shouting. Looking toward the *Sea Otter*, I see her waving at us. It takes a moment to realize what she is yelling: "They are coming back!"

Jamming our heads into the water, we see the dark shapes hurling toward us again. Taking two rapid breaths, we plunge back down into the depths. As I swim furiously, taking pictures of the graceful humpbacks, I think how wonderful life is when one pursues wonder and adventure.

It is not just a matter of chance that I am here. Previously, I spent years perfecting my diving skills and purposefully took courses to enhance my qualifications, such as first aid, life saving, scuba instruction, and equipment repair. I also worked on my physical abilities, practicing long-distance swimming and breath-hold diving. As a U.S. Navy frogman, I spent years leading military dive operations into remote and dangerous locations. I took every possible opportunity to learn more about my chosen trade as a diver. Actively preparing for a dream is the best way to make that goal come true. Of course, opportunity and luck are also heavily involved. Yet, I believe that opportunity is mostly need and skill coming together.

> **Opportunity favors the prepared mind.**
> **—Louis Pasteur**

In order to realize our dreams, it is also critical that we be absolutely reliable. When people depend upon us, we shouldn't ever disappoint them. Many times when the clock alarm rang at 4:00 A.M., I didn't want to get up—let alone arrive at my work station enthusiastic and good-natured. Yet, these are the type of qualities that team adventures demand.

At a depth of forty feet, I aim my camera at the last bull whale (which is about to pass directly beneath me) and shoot the last frame in the camera. Out of film, I capture the last of the exciting moment within my mind. The rapidly swimming whale, fifty feet long, takes only three seconds to hurl under me. I feel a light current from its passage, then Michel DeLoire and I are alone in the vast empty water. Swimming upward we hoot and shout gleefully into our snorkels.

Surfacing, short of breath, I see the whales again surrounding the thirty-two-foot boat. Cindy is running from rail to rail and hollering happily at the whales. The wonderful benefit of pursuing and achieving your dreams is that you can take the people you love with you. A dream shared is the best kind of real-life fantasy. And, just as in a fairy tale, shared-fantasy adventures leads to a purer, happier, and deeper love.

Half an hour later, as I climb back onto the deck of the *Sea Otter*, Cindy hugs me. It is one of the happiest moments of my life.

> **Life has more imagination than we carry in our dreams.**
> **—Christopher Columbus**

Nine

The path of the righteous is like the first gleam of dawn, shining ever brighter till the full light of day. But the way of the wicked is like deep darkness; they do not know what makes them stumble.
—Proverbs 4:18-19

The bright red orb of the sunrise paints the still ocean water with warm, radiant light. In the distance, I see Cindy and Jean-Michel talking at the stern of the *Sea Otter*. I'm in the Zodiac, calmly drifting a quarter of a mile away. There is not yet enough sunlight for filming underwater, so I am taking advantage of a few peaceful minutes alone. It is a good way to start the day. I send up a quiet prayer of thanks to my Maker, and ask Him to watch out for the safety of our team. Diving with humpback whales can be extremely dangerous. The gigantic bulls are very protective around the cows and their calves during the breeding season.

Looking toward the island of Maui, I see a couple jogging on a white sand beach. Ahead of them, two golden retrievers chase each other, barking merrily. The trade winds are blowing lightly from that direction; I can smell the fragrant scent of tropical flowers.

Closing my eyes, I lie back onto one of the Zodiac's rubber pontoons and think about the humpback whales. It is amazing that these huge creatures annually migrate from Alaska to Hawaii and back, yet no one knows the underwater path they take. Whale thoughts are such a mystery for us. Their minds are highly intelligent, but we do not know what they think about. We understand very little about their communication, which covers a wide range of complex squeaks, grunts, and bellows. Each of the humpback males from a specific whale herd or pod

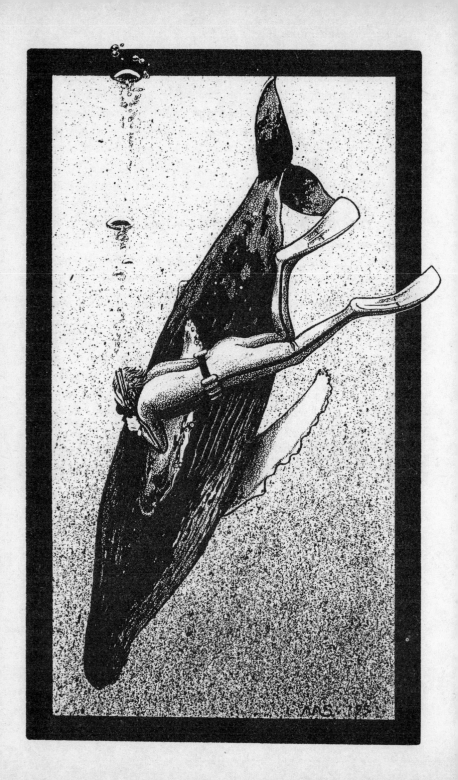

sings the exact same song. The bulls vocalize to charm and captivate the cows. Whale melodies are mournful songs that dance at each end of the musical scale, beginning with prolonged, high-pitched squeaks and squeals that descend into deep rumbling lows. Sometimes the songs echo with a twittering, throat-clearing sound that is like a massive cat purring with the intensity of a fog horn. I hold whale sounds so clearly in my mind that it almost feels as if I am hearing them singing. Startled, I sit up abruptly . . .

The whale song is real! The Zodiac's rubber pontoon, upon which my face is lying, is vibrating softly to the rhythmic sound of a humpback singing nearby. The density of water transmits subsurface sound waves with a lot more punch than air does.

Quickly donning a dive mask, I peer anxiously over the side. Directly beneath the rubber boat, I see the enormous shadow of a bull whale. He is hovering, without movement, in a head-down position. All the leviathan's dynamic energy concentrates on singing his powerful love song.

Grabbing fins and a snorkel, I quietly slip over the side. The water is cool and invigorating, and it resonates with wild music. Taking three quick breaths to clear my lungs of excess carbon dioxide, I then take a final deep inhalation, packing my lungs with oxygen. Jackknifing my body vertically to aid in the descent, I begin swimming silently downward into the deep blue water.

Up close, the humpback is colossal. His whale song engulfs me, magically seeming to fold around my soul. It washes through my body, and I become a part of the bull's music. This is the wonder of whale harmonics; their songs are like a physical force. Beneath the sea, leviathan melodies can be felt as soft, tickling vibrations that play against—and inside—one's entire torso. The deep notes echo strongly through my lungs and sinuses. The high-pitched squeals send long, quivering vibrations along the length of my bones, while the softer gurgles bounce against my skin in a trembling cadence that feels like a body-hugging tickle. Swimming in an ocean of sound and rhythmic vibration, I feel as if I am inside a giant cathedral organ.

Kicking with long strokes of my fins, I sink deeper. The whale's head-down position allows me to approach it unseen. For a moment, I wonder if the whale is bouncing its song off the ocean bottom to enhance its sound and range. The majestic tail floats thirty feet beneath the shimmering surface. Rays of slanting sunlight, filtering down, are bent into long, waving beams that flicker in sync with the undulating water. The sea-softened light washes across the giant humpback, painting it in the radiant colors of the sunrise.

I want to reach out and touch the giant mammal, but I am leery of getting too close. One does not purposefully startle a creature that weighs hundreds of times more than oneself. Swimming just yards away, I wonder what it would feel like to actually touch a singing whale. Would his music reverberate up my arm? Could I actually touch his song?

At sixty feet, the humpback becomes aware of my presence. I am passing the pectoral fin when I see the whale's huge eye rotate in my direction. The pupil is the size of a softball. Seeing my reflection in its shiny dark surface, I marvel at the wild intelligence that is regarding me; then, softly, the whale's song ends on a deep, rumbling low.

The whale's monstrous tail begins to slowly move. With graceful, yet powerful, beats of its fluke, the huge leviathan descends into the dark gloom of deep water. As if in passage with the whale, a cloud passes in front of the sun. In its footsteps walks a long, lingering shadow that casts the depths into a heavy twilight. Suddenly alone, low on breath, I look to the now darkened surface and realize that I am very deep—too deep! The surface is seventy feet away, and panic is knocking at the door. I begin to swim upward urgently, but the world of light seems so far away.

Abruptly, from the dim corridors of my memory, stalks another instant of absolute panic. It comes with a chilling feeling—that first remembered moment of waking up inside a federal prison, of passing from the dimness of deep sleep and awakening to the darkness of a jail cell. Initially, in wild panic, I hoped with all my might that it was just a bad dream; then, I realized that my mistakes were real and there was no escape from the concrete walls and steel bars that would be my reality for three long years.

Swimming vigorously upward, momentarily caught between two worlds (one of shadow and the other of light), I remember the dark gloom of that prison cell. It was such a lonely place, with little music and no laughter at all. To be in prison is to give up many things. I didn't see a sunrise or a sunset for almost a year. It was eighteen months before I could immerse myself in a pool of water, and showers were permitted only every third day. There were no long walks among trees or happy games with friends and family. At first I was completely lost and alone, then I realized it didn't have to be that way. At three o'clock in the morning, two months after my incarceration, I got down on my knees and gave this sinner's life to the Lord. In the darkness of a prison cell, I took my first step back into the light.

> Adversity introduces a man to himself.
> —Anonymous

Now, as I struggle to reach the ocean surface, still twenty feet away, I know I will make it. I watch as the cloud's shadow passes from the sun. Ascending into dazzling sunlight, I gratefully inhale the fragrant tropical air. For a few seconds, I lay on the surface, breathing deeply and basking in the morning sun. What a joy, I think to myself, to be free and so vitally alive.

Climbing into the Zodiac, I take off my fins and mask then look toward the *Sea Otter*. The cabin cruiser is getting underway and motoring directly toward a rainbow.

I hear the crackle of radio static then hear Cindy calling me on the walkie-talkie. "Where have you been?" she asks. "Jean-Michel wants to find whales."

As I reach for the walkie-talkie to answer her, it pleases me greatly that Cindy is here to share my childhood dream of diving with the Cousteau Society. Reaching for the radio, I suddenly feel the rubber pontoon vibrating again. The whale song begins on a high note as I answer Cindy's call. "Tell Jean-Michel he doesn't have to go far. There's one looking for love under my rubber boat."

> Dare to dream, prepare, wear,
> share & repair the dream.
>   —Florence Littauer

Ten

Living moments do not come from committees.
—John Henry Newman

A sixteen-foot-long rubber boat is not very big. Considering that there are only three of us in the Zodiac, one would not expect it to be a logical place for a mutiny. What I am not getting is cooperation. Therry has stopped the outboard and neither he nor Michel DeLoire will let me near it.

"It's not fair," I complain.

"We don't care," the mutineers reply in unison.

After spending all morning chasing whales, we have returned to the *Sea Otter* for more film and fresh camera batteries. Cindy has thoughtfully made me a peanut butter and jelly sandwich however, after loading the other equipment, Therry has motored twenty feet away, so I couldn't have my lunch.

"But I'm hungry." I try throwing myself on their mercy. It doesn't work.

"This boat is on a diet," responds Michel DeLoire.

"The boat is not on a diet—you guys are." I'm getting desperate.

Yesterday, I had located an Hawaiian health food store with all kinds of specialty treats. I personally ground a variety of fresh nuts (macadamia, cashew, and almond) into a super-thick peanut butter. I also picked up a heavy loaf of seven-grain sprouted wheat bread and an assortment of tropical jellies and jams. I really want this sandwich.

Cindy joins in the teasing by dangling the brown paper sack provocatively over the railing. "Don't you want your lunch, Steve?" she teases. "There's a special surprise in here."

I look hopefully at my friends in the boat, but see I'm getting nowhere.

"Shouldn't we be getting back to the whales?" Therry asks Michel as he cold-heartedly shifts the outboard into reverse.

Michel glances at his watch. "Don't worry," he says, patting me on the back. "We'll return for your sandwich in a couple of hours."

In a moment, it will be too late. The gap between the *Sea Otter* and our Zodiac begins to widen. As my panic builds, I know there is only one other option. "Cindy, throw the bag," I shout.

Without hesitation, she hurls the brown sack in a high arc. Therry jams the engine in full reverse. Leaning desperately outward, I claw at the falling paper bag and, just as I barely catch it, Michel DeLoire pushes me over the side of the boat.

Surfacing, I frantically lift the wet paper bag out of the water. Floating on my back, I carefully set the soggy sack on my chest and peer optimistically inside. With a joyous shout, I pull out my sandwich inside a plastic baggy and hold it up triumphantly—it is a zip-lock. Still floating like an otter, I happily open the baggy to find not only a peanut butter and jelly sandwich, but a surprise wrapped in shiny aluminum foil. I set the aluminum surprise package on my stomach for later consideration.

Knowing the guys won't leave me because I am Michel DeLoire's safety diver, I leisurely take a big bite of the sandwich. "Hmmm," I pronounce loudly, "guava jelly."

Michel, who loves guavas, snorts his dissatisfaction—then again, maybe it is his stomach rumbling.

Therry stares curiously at the shiny foil package resting on my tummy. "Aren't you going to open it?" he finally asks.

The foil glistens in the bright sunlight as I purposefully take my time unwrapping it. "Wow, chocolate-covered Maui potato chips!"

"Chocolate what?" Therry maneuvers the boat closer as Michel leans outward for a better look. With obvious irritation, the two dieters unhappily watch me dramatically hold up a large, chocolate-covered chip (Maui potato chips are huge).

With great relish, I eat each chip then lick my fingers and the foil carefully. The dieters are getting really upset. Before it can turn into an ugly situation, Cindy saves the day. "Anyone want a chocolate fudge donut?" she shouts.

Motoring back out to the whales, I grin happily at my friends, who are gobbling a half-dozen chocolate fudge-covered donuts. "I thought you guys were on diets?" I chuckle.

"Donuts are OK for dieters," mumbles Therry, while crumbs fall out of his mouth.

"Donuts are loaded with sugar and fat," I reply.

"That's why they have the hole—it reduces the calorie content," Michel deadpans. "Without the hole, dieters couldn't eat them."

I am preparing to explore that statement when we are interrupted by a breaching whale. The really interesting thing about a whale breach are the dynamics involved. A twenty-five-ton whale can reach breaching speed with only three strokes of its powerful tail. What makes this breach particularly captivating is that it is happening only twenty feet away and it is a baby whale doing the breaching. She circles our rubber boat, throwing her tiny body out of the water seven times in rapid succession. The baby whale is barely the size of a very small school bus, and this breaching business is new to her. Maybe she thinks our inflatable is a whale calf, too, and she is encouraging it to play with her.

Donuts forgotten in favor of cameras, Michel and I hurl ourselves into the water. He leads the descent. On Cousteau filming expeditions, the cinematographer has priority over still photographers. It means I am almost always getting the second-place position. It doesn't help that Michel is able to dive deeper and stay down longer than me; however, he is cheating to do it. Michel is wearing a pony tank, which is a very little scuba cylinder about the size of a loaf of bread. Holding my breath, I follow his small trail of bubbles downward.

The calf is slightly below and ahead of us as she swims back to her mother. I recognize the cow and am instantly pleased. She is a particularly human-friendly whale, affectionately known as Daisy (because of her spotted tail and good disposition). Both whales turn in our direction and slowly swim over for a better look. I watch their eyes tracking Michel DeLoire, then I too come under the whales' scrutiny. The cow's huge eye has a friendly, unconcerned look to it. I imagine I see a touch of pride for the playful calf swimming at her side. I watch the giant eye rotate to check the calf's position as it swims just above her right pectoral fin. It is amazing to look so closely into such a large eyeball. As the giant orb revolves back toward me, I wonder at the mysterious thoughts whirling behind that giant pupil. What is she thinking? Does she know we are only visitors to this underwater world? The thought gives me pause.

Whales live both above and below the water. When swimming on the surface, they see us aboard gigantic ships or in small boats. Do they know these floating machines are lifeless but for us? What must they think of our coastal cities? When swimming close to the Hawaiian islands at night, do they wonder at the lights glittering onshore? Maybe fish are of a far greater concern to them, and we are just tiny, unimportant creatures.

My thoughts about whale perception take off in a new direction with the arrival of the calf. She is swimming straight toward us. Her eyes are wild with curiosity. I see them flicker from Michel to me, then back to Michel. What are these strange creatures? she must be wondering. Do they play? Possibly putting these thoughts to action, the baby whale moves hesitantly closer to Michel.

Without any warning, the peaceful beauty of the moment is shattered by bubbles. There are thousands of them in a huge shimmering curtain that rises out of the depths completely engulfing Michel and me. The startled calf flees in panic back to her mother. Beneath us a giant bull whale continues to express its concern by exhaling another long stream of air bubbles. It is a warning not to be taken lightly. The massive bull weighs fifty thousand pounds—and he is mighty upset!

Bull whales leave bubble wakes as a warning, or a challenge, to other creatures. The huge eye regarding us looks hostile and angry. It is a deep, penetrating glare that sends a shutter vibrating down my spine. I look in alarm from the

angry bull to Michel, who is emitting a small bubble wake of
his own from the pony tank. Could the bull be misinterpreting
Michel's tiny bubbles as a challenge? We do not wait to find
out. Michel and I torpedo for the surface.

Back in the Zodiac, Michel strips off the pony tank. "I
don't think the bull likes my bubbles."

"No kidding," I answer.

We are telling Therry about the encounter with the bull
when we see the whales returning toward the Zodiac. Instantly,
Michel and I hurl ourselves back into the water, less his little
bubble machine. We descend rapidly; the whales are deeper
than before. Daisy and her calf attempt to approach us, but the
bull angrily herds them away. Again, the enraged bull passes
beneath us, only this time the gigantic mammal comes much
closer than before. The threat is very real as he voices his
irritation by releasing a dense stream of large bubbles in an
ascending curtain that momentarily obscures Michel DeLoire
from sight. My alarm is somewhat lessened by the impact of
the giant air bubbles—they tickle as they bounce against my
bare skin. Unable to hold our breath any longer, we nervously
swim back toward the surface, surrounded by buoyant bubbles
bouncing and glittering gaily in the submarine light.

Over the next fifteen minutes, Daisy and her calf make
four more friendly attempts to swim with us, but each time the
bull drives them off—and he seems to be getting angrier with
each encounter. Michel and I are huffing and puffing in the
rubber boat. We are near exhaustion from the repeated breath-
hold dives. The calf surfaces a hundred feet away; again it
heads in our direction. I quickly pull on my fins, but Michel is
winded, probably from too many chocolate donuts. "Go for it,"
he grins. "They're your whales."

"My whales!" I'm ecstatic—and nervous at the same time.
It is wildly exciting slipping into the now chilly water alone.
Without the security of a friend, the depths seem darker and
foreboding. My heart pounds frantically as I swim nervously on
the surface toward the approaching calf. Looking right, left,
and downward repeatedly, I am anxiously wondering where the
bull might be when a giant tail suddenly bursts from the water

right in front of me; the bull is only forty feet away. In stunned amazement, I see the massive fluke rising higher and higher until it towers two stories above me. Then the giant tail slams down in a mighty explosion of water and sound. Frozen in fear, I watch helplessly as the huge fluke strikes the water repeatedly. Each thunderous impact creates dual sound waves. One is underwater; it hammers against my body in a powerful shock wave. The other is an above-water wave that echoes with heavy concussions and half blinds me with a wall of falling water.

Abruptly, the enormous whale surfaces and blows angrily. The bull lies motionless in the water—waiting. Beneath the surface, I nervously peer at the huge eye and, without hesitation, flee back toward the rubber boat. The whale blows one last time then slips below the water.

Returning to the Zodiac, I climb into the rubber boat without any assistance from Michel and Therry, who are both laughing hysterically. Watching my happy companions, I also begin to laugh. Life is more pleasurable when we don't take ourselves too seriously. The laughter spills out of the Zodiac and drifts on the wind to the *Sea Otter*. Hearing it, Cindy waves a greeting, sharing in our pleasure without knowing why.

> **A light heart lives long.**
> **—William Shakespeare**

Eleven

When Jesus spoke again to the people, he said, "I am the light of the world. Whoever follows me will never walk in darkness, but will have the light of life."

—John 8:12

It is two o'clock in the morning, and I am unable to sleep. Cindy left on the sunset flight back to California. She could only join the whale expedition during the two weeks of spring break. Tomorrow, Cindy will be back in her college classroom, studying her lessons but no doubt thinking about whales—and maybe about me.

Lying in bed, I wonder about our future. I already know that I will ask Cindy to marry me; the big question is when (this is not an easy thing for a man to ask). Curled on the nightstand is the flower lei she wore to the airport. In the morning, I will cast the lei into the ocean. It is an ancient Hawaiian custom, a physical promise to return to these tropical islands one day. Lifting the tea leaf-wrapped lei, I inhale the fragrant flowers' delicate bouquet. Dropping it onto my chest, I ponder the wonder of an adventurous life with someone who is as much fun as Cindy.

Outside, I hear the rustle of palm trees swaying in the island trade winds. Several of the long fronds are lightly brushing against the window's wooden shutters. The soft scraping sound blends with the deep-toned chorus of a stand of bamboo trees clunking against each other. The tall hollow trees are thick and old. The bamboo stand echoes with deep reverberations like a giant wooden wind chime. Beneath the music of the wind, there is the deeper rumble of pounding surf. I lean

out the open window and see shimmering waves bathed in moonlight.

My bungalow is nestled amongst the trees, a mere hundred feet from the shore. A few minutes later, I step out its front door. In one hand, I carry Cindy's flower lei; in the other hand are my swim fins. Walking across the white sand beach, I see an almost full moon sailing in a cloudless sky. Its lunar light glistens on the restless ocean. Closer to shore the surf is emitting a faint neon glow of its own. The tumbling action of the wave is exciting the phytoplankton in the water. These tiny life forms (also known as dinoflagellates) contain lyptophase, a substance that emits a soft glow just like fireflies. The cadence of the waves creates a rippling luminescence that pales and fades with each passing breaker.

Walking out into the warm tropical water, I don my fins and begin to swim out. Placing the lei around my neck, I am planning on releasing it out beyond the surf zone. Diving into the white water from the first oncoming wave, I feel the surge ripping Cindy's lei to shreds. Turning to look behind me underwater, I see the spinning flowers washing away, leaving tiny florescent wakes in their passage. I immediately move to part two of my plan—night body surfing!

When swimming out through surf, it is easier to go under the waves. Taking a deep breath, I dunk under the next breaker. The surf is running four to five feet—challenging, but fun-sized waves. Underwater, the bottom is cast in darkness; above me, the waves ripple with their florescent glow. It is here that I begin to hear the whales singing. The humpback sounds are at first faint, but the whale music intensifies as I reach deeper water. Immersed in the whale love songs, I surface just beyond the surf zone, looking to catch my first wave.

In the near darkness, depth perception is difficult to judge. But, as the wave before me builds, I see moonlight radiating through the gleaming wall of water. Using the moon as a reference, I begin kicking vigorously with both fins as the rising swell of water sweeps me upwards. Just before the leading edge of the wave begins to throw out, I launch face-first down the tumbling wall of cascading water. For an instant, I am almost in full free-fall, then my chest plows into the vertical moving surface. Arching my back and reaching out with my right arm creates lift. I begin skimming rapidly across the rushing water. My right arm acts as a rudder; pointing upward, it carries me higher into the racing breaker. Passing over a submerged reef, the wave becomes supercritical; then, the lip before me pitches outward into a perfect revolving tube of water. Momentarily caught inside a spinning vortex, I watch glowing swirls of luminescence play across the fast-moving liquid surface. My outstretched hand knifes into the smooth water, leaving a cometlike wake of neon blue florescent fire. Through the shadowy sheen of the wave's surface, I see the glowing orb of the moon shimmering in the dark water, then the wave collapses into itself, sending me spinning along the bottom.

The underwater surge weaves a glow around each object it washes over. The bottom is alive with swirling trails of florescent light from the phytoplankton. Swimming back to the surface, I shake the water from my hair and eyes and see something I did not know existed. Just before each wave breaks, the trade wind lifts a fine mist of water from the feathery leading edge of the breakers. Caught within the mist, as it momentarily hangs suspended in the wind, is a pale moonbow. The ghostly colors, softly radiant in the mist, evaporate in hardly more than an instant.

For a couple of hours, I play in the surf zone. I watch the moon setting and the night parade of the stars. The whale music swells and fades with its own secret rhythm. Finally exhausted and cold, I ride a breaker back to the shore. On the beach, I see one of Cindy's flowers resting on the white sand. Picking it up, I wish with all my might that Cindy could have shared this magic night with me. One of the truths I have learned about life is that happiness, challenge, and adventure are all enhanced by being shared with a friend.

> Marriage is an adventure in cooperation.
> The more we share, the richer we will be;
> and the less we share, the poorer we will be.
> —Harold B. Walker

Setting the flower back into the water, I watch it swirling back out to sea. In the quiet of the night, I make Cindy a silent promise. *Though you may become my wife, I promise that you will first always be my friend.*

When we treat family as friends and friends as family, we are sharing the best qualities of these relationships with the people we care about the most. Friendships are life's treasures; they define the quality of our existence.

> A man of many companions may come to ruin, but there is a friend who sticks closer than a brother. (Prov. 18:24)

Twelve

For of all sad words of tongue or pen, the saddest are these: "It might have been!"

— John Greenleaf Whittier

A week later, we reluctantly finish our research work with the whales; however, it is not an end to the Hawaiian expedition. Taking a small mountain of equipment to the airport, we fly over to the big island of Hawaii. Part two of the expedition promises to be even more exciting than swimming with whales.

Sunrise the following morning finds me walking across the black tarmac with Michel DeLoire to a waiting helicopter. In the distance stands the imposing presence of the massive volcano, Mona Kea. The mountain is so tall at 13,796 feet (2.6 miles), it creates its own weather. Tropical air, driven by trade winds, swirls up the volcano's steep sides. As the warm air climbs, the temperature drops, forming clouds that drape the upper slopes of majestic Mona Kea. A white veil of nebulous clouds prevents me from seeing the top of the huge volcano. The base of this, the tallest mountain on earth, rests 19,000 feet below the ocean's surface.

Looking to the west, I see the huge volcano, Mona Loa, only thirty feet shorter than her larger sister. Broad-shouldered Mona Loa is the largest mountain on earth. The entire Sierra Nevada Mountain Range would easily fit inside this still active volcano. But it is Kilauea, a much smaller volcano of only four thousand feet, that rivets my attention. Kilauea is erupting!

Staring in awe at the thick cloud of sulfur and steam billowing from Kilauea, I hear footsteps behind me, announcing the arrival of the helicopter's pilot. Clem is from Paris, Texas.

His favorite person in the whole world is John Wayne. Tall and lanky, Clem looks out of place on the big island of Hawaii, wearing boots, frayed jeans, a half-pound silver belt buckle, and a white cowboy hat.

"Shoulda seen the 'cano in '84," Clem says in his thick southern drawl. "She was spewing liquid rock two thousand feet straight up into the air." He hitches up his pants. "So, how close you hombres want to get anyhow?"

"Close as possible," I answer enthusiastically, looking to Michel DeLoire for confirmation. He is holding a sixteen millimeter cinema camera and looking a bit confused.

"Is the pilot speaking English?" asks Michel.

"Huh?" Clem is having difficulty understanding Michel's French accent. "Course I'm speaking English, partner."

Michel looks at me, completely baffled. He has trouble understanding English when it is spoken slowly and simply. Clem's southern drawl is a complete mystery to him, so I quickly repeat Clem's question. "He wants to know how close you want to get to the volcano."

"Oh," Michel nods agreeably. "As close as possible."

Clem happily smacks his hands together. "Good. I've been wanting to peek inside myself . . . Let's saddle up, boys."

"Saddle up?" Michel asks, grabbing my arm. "Stephen, you must translate for me, and what does *peek* mean?"

Michel straps himself into the backseat of the Jet Ranger, while I take the seat next to the pilot. Clem has removed the door from our side of the helicopter to give us an unrestricted view. While the pilot starts the jet engine and begins checking his instruments, I listen to the heavy thump of the rotors as they begin to spin rapidly. The loud whomping sound of the twirling blades stirs a multitude of Vietnam memories in my mind. During the Vietnam War, I did four tours with the Seventh Fleet helping to rescue downed fighter pilots.

"Did he say peek inside?" Michel's voice interrupts my memories. He is hard to hear over the roar of the jet engine and the heavy thumping of the spinning rotors.

"It's just an expression; he isn't really going inside," I shout confidently.

Clem looks over at me and grins. With his radio headset on, he cannot hear what we are saying. He nods at the spare headsets, which Michel and I quickly don. Increasing the rotation of the blades, the helicopter lifts off and begins moving rapidly just above the tarmac. Leaning out of the open door, I watch the ground racing beneath us then look toward the steaming volcano with eager anticipation.

Kilauea had been erupting continuously for four straight years. It is the most active volcano on earth. The lava cone is actually on Kilauea's eastern rift zone twenty-four hundred feet above sea level. Now named Puu O-o, the volcano had fountained lava off and on from 1983 through 1986. For years, the lava had poured out practically on a daily basis. Like a shifting ocean tide, sometimes the lava seeps down the slope, and sometimes it floods. In the process, the lava flow has destroyed sixty-four homes.

En route to the volcano, we pass over a wide area of devastation. Currently, the liquid rock is flowing under a thick blackened crust of hardened lava. Except for wafts of steam rising from the ground, there is not much to see—yet.

The helicopter continues to gain altitude as Clem makes his approach up the steep sides of the eastern rift zone. The trade winds are blowing the column of steam and sulfur inland. "The wind will improve our visibility inside the Puu O-o cone," he says with an eager smile.

Clem is wearing aviator's sunglasses. I can see the reflection of the smoking volcano in the dark panes as I ask, "What do you mean by 'inside?' "

Clem grins wickedly. "Hang onto your shorts, boys. I'm taking this bronc right over the rim."

"What?" I shout.

"Slipping over the rim is the only way we can look down the throat," he answers confidently.

"But what about the helicopter?" I am not believing this is happening. The heat and sulfur of the steam column could stall the engine—and what might it do to the helicopter's passengers?

"This chopper is a rental," Clem replies, tucking the cowboy hat tighter on his head. "It can go anywhere."

We are only five hundred feet from the Puu O-o volcano and slightly above it. From this close, the blackened cone looks huge and foreboding. The thick rim is fractured with a spiderweb of massive, smoking cracks that weep long, crusty tears of yellow and orange sulfur. I quickly glance at the backseat. Michel, always the professional, has his eye glued to the cinema camera's view finder and is rolling footage. Glancing back at Clem, I see the volcano's reflection in his sunglasses growing larger by the second.

"I'll flare the chopper just as we pass over the rim," he shouts. "Should give you a good shot down the throat. You'll only have a second or two."

"A second or two before what?" My heart is pounding against my chest.

"Don't know exactly; never flew into an active volcano before," Clem answers, sounding surprisingly confident. "I expect in that heat column, we're gonna have to go up fast—real fast."

Suddenly it occurs to me that something really outrageous is about to happen—and I'm supposed to be shooting pictures. Leaning out of the helicopter, I quickly focus my thirty-five millimeter still camera. The volcano fills the tiny view finder as I press the shutter release and hold it down firmly. My whole visual perspective of flying into a volcano is through the miniature viewer. The camera's motor drive is rapidly firing three shots a second. I see the sulfur encrusted rim passing barely ten feet beneath the helicopter's skids. The flicker of the shutter frames each exciting moment in a mechanical blink. The heat is incredibly intense, like passing over a blow torch. Inside the cone, I see sheer black walls splattered with blotches of sulfur; then, for an instant (through swirling sulfur smoke), I see the angry red glow of fiercely hot lava. The liquid rock bubbles madly, surging against the blackened stone of the cinder cone. It is a whirlpool of cascading fire that seems to fall away rapidly.

The helicopter rockets upward. Caught in the rising heat column, we are flung straight up, almost eight hundred feet in less than ten seconds. The heat inside the chopper is incredibly intense. Clem banks the helicopter out of the heat column. Immediately, I feel cool wind washing across my face. Lowering the camera, and pulling my head back into the helicopter, I'm astounded to see that my knees are visibly knocking. Beside me, Clem is hooting loudly as Michel leans forward from the backseat. "Can we do it again?" Michel asks politely.

> Some men have acted courage who had
> it not; but no man can act wit.
> —George Savile, Marquis of Halifax

To fully appreciate life, we must be alert and aware of all that is around us. The world is always in flux: things change continuously; events unfold. Either we are swept up in the tide of life or we take charge with a course of our own choosing. With preparation, opportunities can be created. Awareness sparkles when we are blessed with a good education and an open, inquiring mind.

> The world has its own fate and we are part of it.
> Of course, it is partly our business to modify the
> fate of the world. So if we are just spectators, we
> are acting just like a dead weight. We must be
> active actors, because the greatest adventure of
> the universe is the human adventure.
> —Jacques Yves Cousteau

Thirteen

Nothing is what rocks dream about.

—Aristotle

After returning to the airport to refuel the helicopter and reload the cinema camera, Clem takes us back to follow the lava flow on its march to the sea. The liquid rock is mostly traveling underground. Inside the cinder cone, it plunges through the wide crack into a lava tube. The tube carries it down several hundred feet to the Kupaianah Vent, also known as the Lake of Fire.

We approach the Kupaianah Vent with the wind at our back. Beneath us, in a wide crag on the lower slope of the volcano, is a stone caldron several acres across. The Kupaianah Vent really does look like a lake of fire. The surface of the caldron is veiled with a thin crust of blackened rock with flaming red edges. The crust is floating on top of a vast pool of shifting lava.

"We'll circle here for a few minutes," Clem says while holding the helicopter a hundred feet above the burning lake. "Be ready for when it ruptures."

"Ruptures?" asks Michel.

"Yeah, lately the lake has taken to swelling, then it drops a bit," he grins. "Kind of like a clogged toilet trying to flush."

The flushing event begins to happen three minutes later. The lake, which is swelling at the center, abruptly begins to sink toward the southern side. Angry red cracks shatter the blackened crust of rock at the corners, then race jaggedly toward the center. The cracks spread across the lake like a giant spiderweb, then they begin to widen into gapping fissures.

93

Flames leap from the fissures, washing across the ebony surface. The crust, no longer buoyed up by the falling pool of lava, collapses into itself. Wide blocks of crust tumble and sink into the liquid fire. At the lower end of the lake, I notice a broad hole. It is a lava tube twenty-five feet across. The lava is spilling into it in a raging cataract of molten rock. The upper walls of the tube glow a brilliant red from the massive heat inside. As the lake level falls a few feet, the lava flow slows, then the lake's surface smooths, and slowly blackens as a new crust forms.

Heading farther down the side of the volcano, we begin to fly over the residential area, which has disappeared beneath the lava flow. All we see is devastation—a giant field of hardened lava and tumbled rock. Occasionally, we fly over burned-out automobile frames that were swept before the tide of liquid rock like children's toys. There is almost no sign of the houses but for a portion of a stone wall or a little piece of cement walkway. Here and there are small portions of rural streets; the center white lines of the smooth black tarmacs are framed by jagged rock. We pass a lonely stop sign barely poking above the vast lava bed.

The lava is continuing to flow beneath the thick crust cover. Clem discovers a deep fracture, also known as a lava window, and brings the helicopter in close. Hovering momentarily five feet above the crevice, we look down into a bright red cavern to see a subterranean lava fall. The molten lava is plunging in a fiery cascade over a rocky face, washing the cavern with glimmering orange heat. The lava is a dazzling yellow where the rock current is flowing fastest. Rocky ledges at the base of the lava fall and gleam with wet orange fire. Splatterings from the spilling lava hurl across the fiery den in brilliant white splashes. I see all of this in a mere two seconds, before the helicopter must shift away from the intense heat radiating upward through the lava window.

We continue to follow the flow on its march to the ocean. We fly over a ravaged coconut tree plantation. Approaching the shoreline, we see vast, billowing clouds of white steam rising thousands of feet into the air. The lava is pouring into the ocean across a broad front covering a quarter of a mile of rocky shoreline. With the pounding surf breaking away huge steaming chunks of lava, it looks like a war zone. Sheets of spilling lava are turning the ocean surface into a froth of boiling water and exploding liquid rock. Tracers of fluid stone rocket into the air, leaving fiery wakes before splashing into the steaming turbulent water, where they spin madly about with spurts of heat propulsion.

The chopper weaves between the billowing white clouds. I feel the humid heat washing over us. Passing along a sheer wall of spilling red rock, Clem puts the magnitude of the flow into simple perspective. "If a cement truck could haul lava, this flow is the equivalent of more than seventy thousand cement truck loads a day."

Clem stares at the war zone beneath us. "You know, you guys are plumb nuts." He shakes his head to add meaning to his words. "You gotta be crazy to consider diving into that."

Beneath us, the pounding surf breaks a whole section of lava from the shoreline. It falls with a massive hiss into the boiling ocean. Geysers of superheated water erupt into the air, shooting spurts of liquid rock. Wide-eyed, I look at the out-of-control situation and realize that Clem is right—we are out of our minds to consider diving here.

Michel leans forward from the backseat. "Looks like the best place to start our dive operations is near the flow's eastern edge."

I nod voicelessly. It's not that I don't have anything to say; it's just that my mouth has gone suddenly dry. There is no doubt that this will be the most dangerous diving I have ever attempted. For a moment, I wonder if we can really do it. *When we say we can't, we actually mean we choose not to, not realizing it's a choice—"I can't" becomes our reality.*

During times of fear, we often think of the ones we love. Right now my thoughts are on Cindy. I have a responsibility to her, to my team members, and to their loved ones. Certainly, attempting to dive with lava is frightening, yet it can (and has) been done. We are on the threshold of calculated risk. As the expedition leader, I cannot allow events or emotions to rule our course of action. We must approach tomorrow with level heads, with caution, and with respect for the risks we presume to take. This is the required mindset of people who would climb mountains or explore unknown barriers. There is no place on an expedition team for people who act rashly.

To climb a mountain is applied mathematics; each step is calculated against the one before and the one after.

Fourteen

The secret of all victory lies in the organization of the non-obvious.

—Oswald Spengler

Switching off the light in my hotel room, I wonder if I will be able to sleep. Tomorrow promises to be one of the scariest and most challenging days of my life. I am taking a team of friends into extreme danger. As the expedition leader, they rely on me to take charge of the situation. This means extensive planning and research on my part. I must be aware of everything that can go wrong and take steps to prevent any potential disasters. A simple mistake can cost someone his life—or even endanger the entire team. It is a very serious responsibility, so I have been preparing for tomorrow's dive for two solid months. For a moment I consider how it began, in Jean-Michel Cousteau's office on a late Friday afternoon.

The West Coast Cousteau Society office is located on Santa Monica Boulevard in West Hollywood, California. The film capital of the world, West Hollywood is a very interesting place. You never know who you might meet on the street—a familiar face from an old movie or someone from last night's television comedy. I remember staring through Jean-Michel's office window, fascinated by the strangeness of a man below. He was in an alley that parallels Santa Monica Boulevard. The man was tall and very slim. He was wearing black leotards, a black long-sleeved shirt, and black boxer shorts. I could not see his face because he was wearing a white beekeeper's hat with a white mesh veil and a flowing white ribbon tied under his neck. He was busily spinning in tight little circles on roller blades.

He twirled around and through a row of trash cans, bounced up a row of steps, then leapt back down to swirl again around the trash cans. He did this for hours at a time. The weird character was an alley regular.

I turned my attention from the man below to Jean-Michel, who was concluding a telephone conversation with his father, Captain Jacques Yves Cousteau. They are speaking in French, so I have no idea what they are talking about. I have been studying French for a year, but the romantic-sounding language remains a mystery to me. Jean-Michel hangs up the telephone and turns in his chair to face me. "So, Stephen, are you ready for a little adventure?" he asks innocently.

I grin. It is my favorite kind of question.

"I need for you to take a small flying team to Hawaii to film humpback whales," he says casually.

My grin gets bigger. I am liking this conversation more and more.

"Then, I need for you to fly over to the big island of Hawaii. The Kilauea volcano is erupting, and I want you to film the lava flow."

My grin is now out of control; it happily slops across most of my face.

Jean-Michel grins back at me. He is talking so matter-of-factly that it should have been a clue that my boss was setting me up. Jean-Michel loves to tease, so he drops his bombshell, offhandedly. "The lava is flowing into the sea, and we want some underwater footage."

My grin collapses into itself. "What?"

Jean-Michel smiles mischievously. "Captain Cousteau particularly wants you to get close-up footage of the lava flowing underwater."

"Close-up footage? Of lava flowing underwater?" I echo weakly. "How do you film lava flowing underwater?"

Jean Michel boyishly swings his feet up onto the desk. "Well, you begin by going downstairs and getting some of the guys to help you pack up the equipment." Jean-Michel is really enjoying this. "Then, all of you get onto an airplane. When you get to Hawaii, get off the plane and look for an erupting volcano, then follow the lava flow to where the ocean is smoking . . ."

"Jean-Michel!" I interrupt him.

He smiles and stands, happily placing an arm over my shoulder. "Stephen, it is for me to think up the ideas; it is up to you to carry them out. We both know you're going to figure out how to do it. Just be careful."

As I head for the door with my thoughts in a turmoil, Jean-Michel throws a last piece of advice at me. "Diving with lava is going to be scary, but if you plan well, it can be a lot of fun, too."

In my hotel room in Hawaii, I glance over at the clock. It is eleven o'clock in the evening, and I must be up before dawn. I mentally go over the many potential hazards and my strategy for preventing them from endangering the team.

All of the diving will be conducted in a completely exposed surf zone where big breakers regularly pound the shoreline; that means we will be swimming in strong underwater currents, probably with limited visibility, while playing hide-and-seek with rock that is two thousand degrees Fahrenheit. The lava flow itself is very unpredictable. Like a shifting ocean tide, the flowing lava can abruptly surge, creating flash floods of racing molten rock. The volcano's outflow is estimated to be between 350,000 to 500,000 cubic yards a day—enough lava to cover over one hundred football fields with liquid stone to a depth of one yard. Almost daily there are multiple minor earthquakes, occasionally punctuated by a real earth mover. The shoreline where the lava spills into the ocean is very unstable. Landslides are a regular event. Underwater, these sudden slides create strong downward plunging currents that can suck unsuspecting divers to their deaths. Earlier this year, a large submarine landslide flushed a diver down to a depth of over three hundred feet. He barely escaped. After spending a month recovering in a hospital, he now refuses to go anywhere near the lava flow.

So much for the hazards, I think to myself. *Now, what about my plans for preventing them?*

My first consideration is finding the right kind of boat and captain for going into harm's way. This requires a special blend of man and machine because each is only as good as the other's weakest qualities. Usually the condition and layout of the boat reflect the character of the skipper. After some serious searching, I find exactly the right combination of boat and captain.

I chartered a Force Thirty, which is built locally and designed for Hawaii's turbulent waters and heavy surf. *Tsunami* (which means "tidal wave" in Japanese) is an aluminum-hulled, thirty-foot-long cruiser, and with her twin screws she will be quick and agile. It is a boat that can move aggressively in the face of danger. The owner, a barrel-chested Hawaiian named Russell, is a professional fisherman. He often fishes with his boat in big surf conditions, so he knows the wave and current patterns around the lava flow.

I also hire an underwater lava guide, the owner of a dive shop in the town of Helo. Harry has logged over a dozen dives on the lava flow. He is actually an ex-student of mine. We met at the College of Oceaneering, where I taught commercial diving. I know him to be competent and dependable.

Harry is now slightly handicapped. An automobile accident several years ago left him with three fused vertebra in his neck. He is unable to turn his head without rotating his entire upper body. It makes his more animated conversations visually distracting. It pleases me greatly to ask this physically challenged person to join our team.

I've also had extensive discussions with the local volcanologist and with several experienced lava divers. I know the underwater topography of the lava flow; I have driven to the Helo hospital (so I know the way); and I have the radio frequencies for calling in the Coast Guard should we need emergency evacuation or hyperbaric services (a recompression chamber).

Most importantly, my dive team members are all professionals. We are also close friends, and this is the critical key to our safety. As adventurers, we rely on each other to look out for the safety of the entire team. Ours is the close bond of friends who have faced danger together. It is a unique camaraderie built on trust, loyalty to each other, and on hardships overcome through team effort.

Lying in my bed, I snuggle down into the covers, confident that we are ready for tomorrow's challenges. Taking a deep relaxing breath, I am completely unprepared for the sudden arrival of an earthquake.

The bed begins to shake lightly, and I see the clock's red glow vibrating on the nightstand. After a few seconds, the minor earth shaker fades away, leaving me awake for the next couple of hours visualizing underwater earthquakes and land-slides. I am also suspicious about Jean-Michel's casual comment that tomorrow might actually be fun. My last thought before slipping off to sleep is a lingering question that keeps echoing through my mind: Are we really ready?

At first light, after loading the equipment, we trailer *Tsunami* behind a pickup truck with huge, knobby wheels, to a little used boat ramp on the south shore. Most boaters avoid using this ramp because getting out into open water is a very challenging experience. A small cement pier and tiny rock jetty provide little protection, even when the surf is small. Today, of course, large breakers are pounding the south shore. Standing nervously in the parking lot, I watch every third or fourth wave wash over the jetty and smash viciously into the pier.

"What do you think, Russell?" I ask the big Hawaiian.

"Can do, bra." Russell's short answer is not easy to under-stand. Many Hawaiians favor speaking in pidgin, a local blend of English and Hawaiian that uses as few adjectives, adverbs, and modifiers as possible. Russell's speech is even harder to grasp because he is shoveling a jelly donut into his mouth. He glances out at the pounding surf; the waves are cresting at heights of eight to ten feet. "More better, come back by lunch-time," he mumbles, cramming another donut into his face. As Russell bites down, a blob of red jelly squirts out of the donut, sprinkling his T-shirt.

"Why do we have to be back by lunchtime?" I repeat his question for Michel DeLorie's sake. Michel is listening closely, but he is again totally lost in another strange American accent.

"Tide be high, bra, surf much bigger," replies Russell, wip-ing at the jelly globs, effectively spreading them across his white T-shirt.

Russell's plan is simple. All of us get into the boat while it is still on the trailer. Standing at the helm, Russell carefully watches the rhythm of the waves, then he abruptly yells at his cousin, who is behind the wheel of the pickup. The cousin slams the big truck into reverse and quickly shoves the boat trailer down the ramp, then hits the brakes. The Force Thirty slides off the trailer and crashes into the water as Russell fires up both engines, spins the wheel, and goes for full throttle. The stern of the powerful boat digs in, turns 180 degrees, then launches forward. The whole process takes about fifteen seconds before we are plowing into the first oncoming wave.

Russell takes each wave at a quarter angle to reduce the impact. The most interesting aspect of his crashing through the breakers is that there are surfers riding some of the waves. Russell sets his course and leaves it up to the surfers to get out of the way. A couple of them shout and wave as we pass, but somehow I do not think the greetings we are getting are friendly.

As we begin our high-speed run to the lava flow, I ask Russell an important question. "If the surf is going to be bigger when we return, won't it be more tricky bringing in the boat?"

Russell grins. "Yeah, gonna be harder than getting out."

"So, what's your plan?" I am very interested in his answer.

"Same plan as going out," laughs Russell. "Only go much faster."

At 9:00 A.M. we reach our destination and begin motoring just beyond the turbulent water of the lava flow. The boat engine's water inlet temperature is ninety degrees Fahrenheit, and we are still two hundred yards from shore. The water is varying shades of dirty brown with occasional large blotches of black soot. The surface looks like a giant, bubbling mud puddle with floating shadows of dense debris. The bubbles are rising from the bottom, the result of ocean water spontaneously meeting molten rock.

For safety's sake, Michel, Harry, and I will make the first reconnaissance dive. The other two members of the team will stay on the surface. Therry doesn't seem to mind that he is not yet going into the dangerous water. The inlet temperature is now 105 degrees. Russell carefully maneuvers the boat closer to shore.

Yesterday from the air, the lava spilling into the ocean looked really scary.

This morning, from the up-close perspective of a small boat, I see that the lava flow is downright terrifying—it looks like a futuristic war zone. Before me, across its half-mile front, tremendous amounts of molten rock spill into the ocean. In a few places, the lava weeps slowly into the bubbling water, but mostly the fiery rock is gushing forth in thick globs or in fast flowing streams. A billowing wall of sizzling steam rolls off the turbulent water. At the heavy flow points, the liquid rock is so hot the ocean water instantly flashes into superheated vapor. I watch a wave break off a large chunk of steaming lava; it falls, hissing loudly into the water; then it explodes, hurling long liquid tracers of lava through the air. One of the tracers falls back into the water only fifty feet from the boat; it momentarily spins about, spewing out spits of steam like an errant firework.

Russell reverses the engines and motors back out, looking for cooler water.

"It is really out of control today," offers Harry, our guide, echoing my thoughts exactly.

"Think it's safe enough to dive?" I ask seriously.

"Nah," he shrugs, awkwardly turning his whole body from the shoreline toward me. "It's never safe; that's why so few people have ever dove the lava flow."

"This is going to be more fun than diving with the salt water crocodiles," laughs Michel as he begins suiting up.

"Is he kidding?" asks Harry. "He hasn't really dove with crocodiles?"

"Yeah, last year in an Australian river," I answer. "He filmed a twelve-foot-long saltwater crocodile from only two feet away."

"From inside a sturdy steel cage, no doubt," chuckles Harry.

"Actually," replies Michel nonchalantly, "I didn't like how the cage bars restricted my filming, so I went into the water without it."

"Wow," Harry says, impressed. "Would you do it again?"

"No. Crocodiles have very large teeth and move fast. I wasn't being very smart." Michel picks up the underwater cinema camera. "Are we ready?" he asks calmly.

I glance at the engine's water inlet thermometer; it is back down to 101 degrees. "Let's rock and roll," I say with more enthusiasm than I am feeling.

Stepping to the side of the boat, I leap overboard. It is like jumping into a giant Jacuzzi, with a wet suit on. The hot water instantly fills my rubber suit and half floods my dive mask. Some of the hot, sulfur-tainted water trickles up my nose, but I do not pause to clear the mask; instead, we urgently swim straight down. We already know that the water is hottest near the surface. Quickly submerging to a depth of thirty feet, we level off in the cooler, yet still hot, water. My wrist-mounted thermometer is indicating eight-five degrees. The water feels muggy, like wading through a hot swamp. Checking my compass and the direction of the sun, I orient us toward the shoreline, and we begin our approach.

At this depth it is very murky; we pass through dark underwater clouds of soot and ash. Closer to shore, the sunlight dims to a dull red glow that waivers and fades to darkness with each passing soot cloud. I keep glancing at the compass, yet it is hardly needed. The lava flow is producing a pounding cascade of underwater sound. It pulsates before us in loud crackling shock waves, as rock is being ripped, torn, and blown apart. As we get closer, the crackling, tearing reverberations intensify. I can feel the sudden passage of each shock wave as it strikes the rubber covering my ears.

I am doing continuous buddy checks. Michel is swimming strongly with his camera to my left. I see Michel's face plate sweeping side-to-side as he eagerly looks for the first sign of liquid lava. On my right, Harry swims oddly because of his fused neck. He is doing extraordinarily large kicks with his fins. Each of the long strokes causes his body to roll off-keel. He does this purposefully to create the rolling effect that permits him to look to each side. During one of his partial revolutions, our eyes momentarily lock; he smiles then rotates away from me.

Checking my compass, I see that the needle is swinging wildly. The liquid metal ores in the lava flow make the compass all but useless. I look for the sun to check my direction, but in the shadowed twilight of the underwater soot clouds, it is completely hidden. I try determining our heading by listening to the concussion of sound—and that is when I realize the terrible noise is now coming from beneath us. We are passing directly over a main part of the flow. The water becomes hotter and more active. There are abrupt heated currents swirling up from the depths. I can feel myself sweating inside the wet suit; it is a strange sensation underwater. Swimming more slowly, peering fearfully into the dark water below, my mind paints its own terrifying images of the inferno that is happening directly under us.

Looking forward, I see a wall of darkness—a soot cloud vast in its dimensions. I am reluctant to swim into it. The other divers and I have gotten slightly separated. I have the strongest feeling that we could completely lose each other inside that dark hovering cloud. Holding up my fist, I signal the other divers to stop. The situation is just too dangerous to continue. I look to Michel and shake my head side-to-side, then jerk my thumb back in the general direction of the boat; he nods his agreement.

As we are swimming back out, I hear a deep rumble, then a far-off sound of rolling thunder. Somewhere behind, or deep below us, a major avalanche is occurring. I am thankful not to be near it as the water around us begins to brighten. Seeing faint sunlight glimmering through the water, I slightly alter our course. I inhale deeply through my regulator; life feels good. In the distance we begin to hear a clanging sound. It is Therry beating two metal pipes together from the back of the boat. The ringing noise is calling us home as we swim eagerly toward it.

We spent an entire month trying to film the lava flow underwater without success. The situation was just too dangerous.

In life we cannot accomplish everything we seek to do. Yet, the most important thing about reaching for dreams or goals is the journey on which they take us. It is what we learn along the way. We weave all of our experiences, whether they are accomplishments or failures, into a tapestry upon which we build our character. This becomes the fabric of our strengths—or of our weaknesses. It all depends upon our attitude about life and about ourselves.

To be truly happy we need to see ourselves in a positive light. This is part of the wonder of a Christian commitment. Our focus is toward what is good. From goodness comes the strength of Truth. These are good foundations upon which to build an adventurous and satisfying life.

When facing death, some will wonder, Did my life have meaning or purpose? Others may regret the things they didn't do. As an active Christian adventurer, these are not questions I will have to ask myself.

> **To Be is to live with God.**
> —Ralph Waldo Emerson

Fifteen

*The Bible is alive, it speaks to me; it has feet, it runs after me;
it has hands, it lays hold on me.*

—Martin Luther

I am again sitting in Jean-Michel's office. Outside his
window a nighttime rain beats lightly against the glass. Multicolored neon lights shimmer through the slick wetness. The
headlights of passing cars on Santa Monica Boulevard are
rimmed in sparkling halos of misty white brightness. Just back
from Hawaii, I stare anxiously at the rain rivulets running
down the window pane and hope the weather will not delay
Cindy's flight. She is flying in for the weekend, and I cannot
wait to tell her about the lava dives.

"Are you listening to me?"

Jean-Michel's voice snaps my attention back to him. "Yes,
boss," I reply, sitting up more attentively in my chair.

Jean-Michel impatiently taps a pencil on his desk. "What
was I saying then?"

"That Michel DeLoire forgot something," I reply, pleased
to know the answer. Yesterday, Michel DeLoire flew directly
from Hawaii to Papua New Guinea to join the wind ship
Alcyone, the Cousteau Society's newest research vessel.

"Would you like to know what Michel forgot?" Jean-Michel
asks. Alarm bells are suddenly going off in my head. Am I the
one responsible for the forgotten item? "What did he forget?"
I nervously inquire.

Jean-Michel consults his notebook. I watch his index finger going down a brief list, which is not only upside down from
my perspective; it is also in French. Lacking any visible hints,
I anxiously await my fate with a pounding heart.

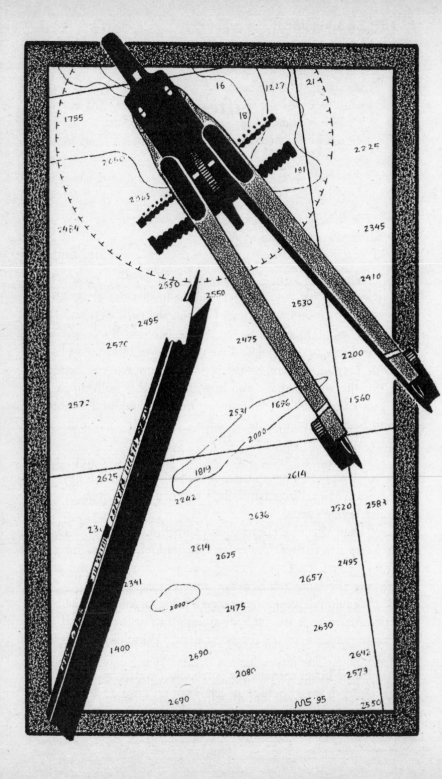

Jean-Michel's finger pounces on the missing item. "You!" he exclaims with great drama.

"Me, what?" I ask imploringly.

"You," Jean-Michel says, pointing an accusing finger at my chest. "You are what he forgot."

"He forgot me?" I want to feel relief; instead I am feeling slightly confused.

"Yeah, you." Jean-Michel grins, then slides an airline ticket across the desk. "You're leaving for Papua New Guinea tomorrow evening at eight o'clock."

"But, but . . ." I sputter hopelessly, "Cindy's arriving tonight."

"Good, you're going to need her help."

"I am?" In my mind, all the fun things I've planned to share with Cindy over the weekend are fading.

Jean-Michel hands me a lengthy telex. "It seems *Alcyone* needs a few things."

I quickly scan the telex, which begins with the sentence, "Dear Stephen, you will be welcome aboard *Alcyone*, if you bring the following . . ." What follows is a three-page shopping list.

Four days later, I am again looking out a window at a nighttime rain. A bright stab of lightening reinforces that this is not a gentle California rain shower. This is a tropical thunderstorm, eight thousand miles away from the comfort of Jean-Michel's office. I am aboard the research vessel *Alcyone* and sailing straight into a massive thunderhead. Glancing at the revolving light bar on the radar scope, I see the towering clouds painted in angry red light. The wind ship is sailing straight into the heart of the storm. Fortunately, at the ten-mile range on the scope, I see we should hit clear water in another hour.

It is my very first watch aboard the wind ship and other than being slightly seasick, I feel terrific. At the helm of a world-famous research vessel, with a course set for adventure, I am living out my childhood dream. Watching heavy raindrops pelting the wind ship's plate glass windows, I turn up the music on the stereo. The Beach Boys are singing "California Girls," which sets me to thinking about Cindy.

Our big weekend date lasted less than eighteen hours. We spent the entire time packing twenty-two boxes of supplies. We went to the airport together, she with her light carryon bag, and me with my mountain of luggage. Dropping her off at the domestic terminal, I collected a hug and a wisecrack. Cindy assured me that, on the dating scale, this weekend should not be considered the highlight in our relationship.

"Because we spent the entire time packing supplies?" I ask unhappily.

"No, because you're going off on another fun adventure, and I'm going back to school." Cindy punches my arm to add impact to her words.

"Hey, school can be exciting, too," I offer defensively.

"You want another punch?" Cindy playfully draws back her fist, but instead of hitting me, she leans her head against my chest and fakes a sniffle. It is amazing how well Cindy works my emotions. Before I know it, I'm apologizing for unfairly going off on another adventure. Then, I grab a hug and go alone to the international terminal.

On the *Alcyone's* bridge, the Beach Boys' song comes to an end, but my thoughts about Cindy continue. Her comments about adventure have set me to thinking. In a quality relationship both people must share equally. Since Cindy and I are both adventure hounds, it is only fair if I ensure that she gets her quota of excitement, too. One of the challenges of love, or friendship, is to always share. Sharing improves everything it touches.

A thick bolt of lightening strikes the ocean off to the starboard side. A few seconds later, the vibrato of deep rolling thunder momentarily blends with the Beach Boys' song "Good Vibrations." The powerful, uplifting beat fits my mood perfectly. Humming along with the music, I step to the chart table to check our position. Our destination is the Bismarck Archipelago, a long chain of lush tropical islands in the northern waters of Papua New Guinea. Staring at the chart under my hands, as I prepare to plot the *Alcyone's* course, I realize that our lives are also like a charted course. In life, we are always coming from somewhere and going somewhere else. Realizing that this is basically a never-ending journey, it is not the single destination that counts as much as the quality of the passage.

As a Christian, I have strong motivations to live each day with the right focus. My daily goal is to make positive choices and to do good work. The chart in my hands points out the various marine hazards, such as rocky shallows and underwater reefs. With this map, I can easily navigate the *Alcyone* past the obstacles—as long as I know where I am in the first place. Being a Christian gives me my daily starting point. The chart I use for my life is found in the Bible in Mark 12:30-31. It is here that Jesus is asked, "Of all the commandments, which is the most important?"

> "Love the Lord your God with all your heart and with all your soul and with all your mind and with all your strength." The second is this: "Love your neighbor as yourself." There is no commandment greater than these. (Mark 12:30-31)

By following these two simple laws, we are automatically on the right course. We always know exactly where we are and where we are going. Any decision in life can be weighted against these two laws, making the correct answer easy to find.

Later that night, Therry relieves me at the helm. Going below, I silently step into the captain's cabin and get into the lower bunk. Quietly slipping under the covers, I let the rolling motion of the ship lull me to sleep.

Early the next morning, the *Alcyone* arrives at Long Island. We anchor in a quiet cove with tall palm trees leaning out over the water. The island is volcanic in origin, rising rather abruptly out of the ocean during the eighteenth century. It has extremely steep sides that lead up to a gigantic crater seven hundred feet above sea level. Inside the crater is a huge lake, and inside the lake is an active volcano. Mut Mut happens to be the newest volcano on earth, having risen out of the lake less than three years ago. Getting to it requires a seaplane, which lands at our anchorage an hour after sunrise and taxies up to the stern of the wind ship.

The Cousteau seaplane is called *Papillon*, which means "butterfly" in French. Sitting beside the pilot is an Australian scientist named Patty. She is here to study the flora growing on the juvenile volcano. The seaplane ferries the Cousteau team up to the lake, three people at a time. It seems a strange journey to fly upward alongside the island's sheer cliffs. We discover at the top of the crater a wide lake with another island in the middle of it—the shores of which are six hundred feet above sea level.

In awe of our unusual journey, Michel DeLoire exclaims in French, *"Incroyable, c'est une île dedans une île* [Incredible, it is an island inside an island]."

I nod in agreement, unsure how to express (in French) the wonder I am seeing.

What makes Mut Mut particularly unique and of acute scientific interest is its near isolation. People have no access to it because of the surrounding island's sheer cliffs.

The lake is scalding hot with temperatures ranging from 120 to 170 degrees Fahrenheit; therefore, there is as yet no known active marine life in the vicinity of Mut Mut. Fortunately, the hotter water is near the bottom where the heat is radiating upward from the volcano's foundation. The surface will be cool enough (120 degrees) to land the *Papillon*.

We land a short distance from Mut Mut, where the water is cooler, then taxi across the hotter water to a black gravel beach at the volcano's base. The *Papillon's* pontoons come to rest in only a foot of water. We scurry along the pontoon, then dash quickly across the last couple of yards of hot water to the beach. Rapidly, each of us discovers that the gravelly beach has hot, and not so hot, spots. Finding a solid rock ledge that feels almost cool to the touch, I set down my equipment, then I scurry back to the *Papillon* to collect more gear.

Unlike Kilauea, this juvenile volcano is not releasing lava. Instead, Mut Mut is slowly growing. The lava inside causes it to swell upward approximately two to three inches each day. Its sloping sides weep steam and smoke from the intense heat contained within. Yet, on this visibly hostile surface, there is life.

Visiting birds (or strong trade winds) have left seeds, which find root in rocky nooks and crevices. It seems impossible, but amongst the dark smoking rocks, here and there, are green sprigs growing toward the sunlight. On the black gravelly beach is where the most plant life is found. There are mosses, long-stemmed grass, and a few small ferns growing in the shade of steaming rocks.

While Patty takes samples for later study, I set about doing some exploring on my own. I feel Mut Mut's heat radiating through my thick boots as I scramble up three hundred feet to the volcano's rim. The miniature cone's interior is mostly smoking rock rubble. Circling the rim, I hunt for new vegetation. Behind a rocky ledge, sheltered from some of the heat, I discover a three-foot-tall, broad-leaf plant. Squatting down, I pause to admire this deceptively sturdy plant. Its fragile roots wrap in a tight weave around sharp-edged rocks, anchoring the delicate main stem. There is no visible soil, yet the plant is thriving. It is a triumph over adversity.

I am quite proud of the little courageous plant as I lead Patty to see it. Her squeal of delight makes me feel almost like a proud father. In my mind, the plant and I have bonded; therefore, imagine my shock and surprise when Patty pounces on the plant, ripping it up by the roots.

"What have you done?" I shout in dismay.

Patty looks truly surprised. "Why, I'm taking a sample," she says, shaking gravel from the torn roots.

"That's not a sample—it's the whole plant." I stare at the shredded roots and torn stem.

"It's called science, silly." Patty is clamping the plant into a wooden press to preserve its shape.

"Why couldn't you just take a leaf or two? Surely, that would have given you the data you need." I'm beginning to wonder if I am being silly, making such a big deal over a plant.

"Well," Patty says as she stands and brushes off her hands, "I need to know its height, weight, and bio-mass." She sounds as if she is addressing a fairly dense student. "From the roots, we will do mineral analysis, determine water content, and check acid levels."

Now, I'm truly feeling silly, but then I remember how good the plant made me feel. As the scientist finishes tightening the screws on the wooden press, I see a few crushed leaves and bruised stems drooping beyond the wooden sides. It makes me mad. "I'm not buying it, Patty."

"I beg your pardon, but when did you become a scientist?" Patty is getting fired up herself.

"Isn't the main thrust of your investigation to examine the growth of life on Mut Mut as an isolated land mass? And did you not just rip up the only plant of its kind that we've been able to find on the entire island? In fact, won't that potentially upset the parameters of your study?" I'm just getting into swing when Patty angrily interrupts me.

"OK, I promise not to rip up any more plants; I'll only take small samples." With that, Patty goes off to a more remote side of Mut Mut.

Sitting down on the hot stone, I stare at what remains of the shredded roots. Sometimes people do things under the justification of a cause; however, this does not automatically make them right. In labs around the world, innumerable helpless animals suffer in the name of science. Maybe it is hard to argue with this practice when human lives are at stake. But, what about the cosmetic company scientist who will clamp a rabbit's eyelids open and saturate the helpless animal's eyes with harsh chemicals just to see if a new hair spray will irritate a person's eyes? The cosmetic company will continue to abuse this defenseless animal on a regular basis to see if cancers or sties eventually form—all in the interest of selling a cosmetic product.

Looking inside the crevice, I see that there is still a bit of the main root left. I pour a little water from my canteen onto the damaged root in the hope that the plant might regenerate itself. Heading back down toward the beach, I see Patty. She has both hands wrapped around a clump of grass, which she is jerking vigorously. In the middle of the clump is a delicate purple flower. Finally pulling the entire clump free, she dumps the grass and flowering plant onto the press. In the frenzy of her activity, she doesn't notice the flower as it is picked up by the trade winds. It swirls in the breeze, then settles in a nearby volcanic crack. Continuing my way down the mountain, I unscrew the top of my water bottle, then gently pour the remainder of its contents onto the flower. I doubt that my little bit of water will make much of a difference, but it makes me feel good.

Pausing to watch Patty vigorously twisting the screws to her wooden press, I think that some researchers can be so focused on their studies that they are blind to the true wonder that is about them. Where they may see bio mass, I see the beauty of God's creation.

> A little science estranges men from God,
> but much science leads them back to Him.
> —Louis Pasteur

Sixteen

Faith is the bird that sings when the dawn is still dark.
—Sir Rabindranath Tagore

Our next stop is at Tench Island, which means "rock." It is an appropriate name for this tiny island. Barely bigger than a city block, the little island supports a primitive, yet picturesque, village of fifty-five people. It is a quiet place. There are no engines or even any electricity here. Tench is an isolated island where people work and live out their entire lives, yet it totally lacks the mechanical sound of industry. Walking one of the jungle paths, I hear only the sound of children's laughter against a background of gentle breaking surf and the rustle of wind in the palm trees. There are birds everywhere, mostly gooneys, sitting on or walking about the ground. They are unimpressed by my presence and refuse to budge from my path, so it is I who moves out of their way.

Stepping from the dense jungle onto a hidden white sand beach, I find a group of children playing. One of them has a colorful bird on his shoulder, which squawks loudly at my intrusion. While the big yellow bird eyes me suspiciously, I watch the kids pushing stick canoes into the water. One of them offers to share his lunch of taro root chips with me. The fried taro chip is as thick as a pancake and each one takes several minutes of industrious chewing. The bland chip's only flavor is the acid bite of charcoal. I gratefully decline a second offer of taro root chips and silently promise myself never to accept another one. Instead, I give the kids my apple, which is something they have never seen before. The shiny fruit passes from child to child to yellow bird, then back to me. I give my

piece to a gooney. Never having had an apple before, the gooney spits it on the ground and stomps on it.

The first dive of the expedition is in the village's underwater gardens. The gardens are found just beyond the surf zone in six to ten feet of water. The villagers define the boundaries of each garden with shallow walls built of coral rubble. Inside the small enclosures are giant clams, some of them weighing over four hundred pounds. The villagers search the underwater reefs for juvenile clams, which they carefully move into their gardens. Some of these clams are so old they are passed from grandfather to father to son. Except for the bamboo and grass huts, a hollowed-out canoe, and a shell necklace, this will be the children's only inheritance.

The villagers will harvest a clam only during special holidays or in times of severe need. Unfortunately, these people, who have so little, sometimes fall prey to passing thieves in the night. Taiwanese fishermen come under the cover of darkness. With knives they sever the main muscle that closes the giant clam's shell. Taking only the severed muscle, they abandon the rest of the animal to die. The clam, unable to close its protective shell, will be ravaged by scavenger fish and reef sharks. In the morning, the villagers will only find the empty shell.

It always amazes me how greedy people find ways to justify their needs above the rights of others. For the thieves, the clam's muscle will make a small meal for just a few. For the village, the giant clam would have been a plentiful bounty from the sea, a meal eaten with great ceremony and appreciated by all.

> Woe to those who go to great depths to hide their plans from the LORD, who do their work in darkness and think, "Who sees us? Who will know?" (Isa. 29:15)

Later, back aboard the *Alcyone*, I am at the stern when the village medicine woman arrives in an outrigger canoe. As the team medic, I cannot resist sharing some of my medical supplies with her. In return, she gives me a toothless smile and a big coconut leaf full of taro root chips.

It is almost sunset before I can unload all of the chips on unsuspecting crew members; then, as the sun sinks toward the

horizon, I slip over the side with one of the Cousteau underwater scooters. We will be sailing after dinner, and this will be
our only opportunity for a night dive. I am planning on using
the scooter for some fast underwater exploring to find the best
possible filming location. Triggering the scooter, I head out on
the surface for deeper water. A minute later, I turn to get my
bearings and am awed by a spectacular sight.

A hundred yards away, the *Alcyone* lays at anchor with
Tench Island looming behind her. From the water, I see the
radiant colors of the sunset washing over the wind ship's graceful hull and tall metal sails. The futuristic-looking vessel almost appears to be a visiting spaceship caught in the bright
halo of a search light. I see the rest of the team readying their
diving gear. Dressed head-to-toe in silver wet suits, they look
like exotic space visitors. Their metallic wet suits shimmer with
reflected light as they move about the deck. In the surrounding
water, many of the villagers are paddling hollowed-out canoes.
A torch burns at the bow of each outrigger. The yellow dancing
flames circling the research vessel lend a strange primal con-
trast to my mental spaceship image of the *Alcyone*.

Placing the scuba regulator into my mouth, I again trigger
the scooter and begin a rapid descent. Below me, all is cast in
shadowed darkness. Switching on the scooter's head lamp, the
bright beam startles a twenty-pound tuna. The silver fish flees
downward as I follow in high-speed pursuit. Beneath me, the
scooter's beam paints a shallow reef with its wide arch of brilliant light. Under the artificial glow, the rich colors of the reef
leap forward. I see white soft sponges that look remarkably like
snow banks. Skinny, long-armed, starfishlike, brown creatures
called crinoids lean out into the slight swaying surge; their
slowly waving spindled arms resemble leafless trees in a gusting
wind. It is as if I am passing into a winter wonderland. Multicolored corals glisten like spilled candy on a bed of sparkling
white sand. The dazzling display reminds me of Christmas.
Flying closer to the reef, I pass over a teddy bear starfish with
its brown body and cream-colored legs. The dive pleases and
fascinates the kid in me.

Quickly returning to the wind ship, I lead the team to what would be known by all as Christmas Reef. The night dive becomes a holiday event, a celebration of living color.

A couple of days later we arrive at Manus Island, which has a thriving population of thirty thousand people. This is a busy, crowded place with constant noise. Everywhere there are the unmuffled sounds of motor scooters, boat engines, and diesel trucks that belch black clouds of acid smoke. Radios blare from taxis, bars, and from thatch huts. The street gutters are littered with trash and debris. The island's small bustling towns have movie theaters and video rental stores. From the billboards, I see that the number-one movie star in Papua New Guinea is Sylvester Stallone as Rambo. It is beneath one of the Rambo billboards that we meet Job, the man we have come to interview.

Job is not an appealing person to look at. He is dirty and wearing torn clothes. Empty beer bottles cover the trash heap at the side of his dilapidated hut. It reeks of rot and decay, as does the man himself. Job is a cripple, a feat of his own accomplishment.

During World War II, intense fighting raged on Manus Island. The retiring armies left excess munitions in large abandoned heaps. Job has spent years raiding the old munitions dumps for their explosive powders, which he converts into underwater bombs to kill fish.

Job calls his improvised explosive devices "Du Pont Lures." He finds a fish-filled reef and tosses a homemade bomb into the water. The explosion kills all the fish within a wide area; only a small number, can be recovered by Job, particularly in his crippled state. Five years ago, one of the bombs went off when he was preparing to throw it. The explosion took his arm and one eye and peppered him with shrapnel. I look at him without sympathy. He is still relentlessly bombing the reefs. In my mind, I vividly remember the devastated reef we saw only yesterday.

Closing my eyes, I am again swimming along the length of a shallow reef. It is devoid of fish and crustaceans; even the delicate algae are brown and dead. The once beautiful corals now lie in shattered heaps. The bombs gouge large holes in the reef, leaving numerous fossil falls of tumbled, broken rock that have turned living corals into rubble. I could not help comparing this sick and dying place with the startling beauty of Christmas Reef. I feel the anger beginning to well up within me.

Opening my eyes, I again look at the broken man who wantonly causes all this havoc and destruction. Suddenly, I realize that the explosives have left scars above the water as well as below. This man's mind and body mirrors the destruction of the reef and, like the reef, the man suffers. My anger fades in an instant. To save the reef, the first step might be to save the man. If left to his ways, Job will not change, nor will the reef get the opportunity it needs to heal. Looking at the broken man I see what is missing in his life—hope.

> Hope deferred makes the heart sick, but a longing fulfilled is a tree of life. (Prov. 13:12)

Glancing back at the outskirts of the small town, I see shadows of the once beautiful island, now buried under piles of industrial waste. The destruction Job practices underwater is echoed here on the land by others who are just as uncaring. For a moment, I have an overpowering sense that something important is missing in this bustling island town. I see traffic congestion on the main street with its pall of acrid smoke. I see a group of drunk men arguing outside of a bar; above them hangs a rusted movie marquee, missing several letters. Then it hits me. On the taxi ride from the harbor, through the middle of town to Job's shack, I have not seen a single church.

People who lack spiritual hope live mostly for the present. Many of them do not plan for, nor care much about, future generations. Their main motivation in life is to take and not to give. When people lack a close personal relationship with God, and with each other, the ways of man are set free to ravage without moral restraint. Greed is unleashed upon the land and upon its helpless creatures. Yet, hope, even in the midst of destruction, is never lost. I know that somewhere on this island, there are Christian missionaries teaching that with forgiveness comes hope. Christian fellowship recovers people's lost dreams and restores happiness where there is none.

> Dreams and beasts are two keys by which
> we find out the keys to our own nature.
> —Ralph Waldo Emerson

Seventeen

The Bible should have as important a place as the TV set in our American homes. Our future progress may well depend not so much on our productive and technological genius as upon our moral awareness.

—Clifford F. Hood

Our next stop is at Wuvalo, the last and one of the most isolated islands of the Bismarck Archipelago. It is here, on this quiet, beautiful island, that I discover the actual device that is changing these simple island people from their peaceful ways. The instrument of their change is brought out only at night. Several men carry it into the middle of the village like some secret treasure. The people hurry to get the best places to pay homage to this new, alluring wonder.

In stunned fascination, I watch the impact of television on primitive people who are totally unprepared for the high-tech invasion of twentieth-century entertainment. The television arrived several months ago, along with a gasoline generator for power and a VCR to feed it. Every ten days an island trading boat arrives. Besides bringing essential supplies, the boat also serves as a video rental store.

The village chief, standing beside me, proudly confides the wisdom of his decision to purchase the television equipment with community funds. "It is like we have joined the rest of the world," he whispers, eyes fixed on the television monitor. "The movies unlock the mysteries of what is really happening everywhere else," he says, caught up in cinematic awe.

The movie the villages are watching is *Scar Face*, with Al Pacino. This is an extremely violent movie about the cocaine

trade in Florida. On the glaring orb of the television screen, we see a simple man from a Cuban rural background immigrating into the United States with nothing to his name. He appears to be the kind of person these people can identify with. Through the drug trade, he rapidly acquires money, power, fast cars, a beautiful wife, and an expensive home. He also happens to kill people—a lot of people.

As I look at the villagers, all but hypnotized by the crime drama, I wonder if they realize that the only time the main character, Scar Face, smiles is when he is hurting someone. Do they see the evil that the drug trade represents? No. Instead, they appear to be caught up in the Hollywood magic of bright city lights, drama, and intrigue.

When the movie ends, the young boys run amongst the palm trees pretending to shoot one another with machine pistols. By an open fire, a group of men are talking excitedly about a scene in which a man is attacked with a chain saw. A couple of the smaller kids are rapidly pushing toy wooden canoes through the sand and making race-car noises.

The chief looks at all the activity and grins proudly. "Next week the boat is bringing us a pirated copy of *Rambo*," he says with a broad smile. "The movie is hard to get. I have to pay double."

Walking down to the beach, I shove the *Alcyone's* rubber Zodiac out into the dark water. Taking a last look back at the village, I see three boys silhouetted before a fire. Two older boys are holding down a toddler and pretending to cut off his limbs with a chain saw. The little boy is crying at the harsh treatment; the older boys are laughing maliciously.

Motoring back out to the *Alcyone*, I think about the tremendous impact television is having on these people. Undoubtedly the youths will want to move to the big cities where they can experience what they've seen. In their minds, they may be eagerly thinking of trading in their hollowed-out canoes for fast cars, and their bamboo huts with star-filled nights for apartments in neon-lit cities. In the near future, the primitive social fabric of this tightly knit island society is probably going to unravel beyond repair.

That night, in my cabin aboard the wind ship, I ponder the impact television is having on American youths. We tend to judge ourselves by those we see around us. Television programming adds a new dimension or standard to these values. In television dramas and music videos, we often see attractive people exploring the dark edges of what is not normally acceptable behavior. Television is more than just a window into a fantasy world where real life merges with creative imagination. It is a medium that allows people in the movie trade to present their own thoughts and values on life. Though their teachings may be distorted, or even malicious, the message will always be presented in the most alluring and attractive way. Deception is most effective when it pretends to be something that is supposedly good. Why else would Satan masquerade as an angel of light?

As a reflection on the power of cinema, ask a young person who is a bigger hero for most kids, George Washington or Indiana Jones? In my own surveys, I find that the fictitious character, played by an actor, beats out the Founding Father of the United States by a factor of approximately ten to one.

Every day more than thirteen hundred teen-agers attempt suicide. It is the number-three killer of teen-agers in America. Television values weigh heavily on all of us. In truth, television is but an electrical box in front of which the average North American youth sits idly for twenty-two hours a week. What a loss, when real life adventure is always waiting just outside the front door. The short time of our youth is when we are the most creative, imaginative, and energetic. How horrible to waste all that youthful wonder and energy—just sitting idly in front of a box.

The next morning, what begins as a regular day of Cousteau underwater adventure, suddenly becomes the event of a lifetime. We encounter three killer whales hunting amongst the reefs of Wuvalo Island. For eight incredible hours, the Cousteau crew splits into twin teams to take two-hour shifts diving with these orcas. My team is just exiting the water as Jean-Michel's team takes over for the last dive of the day. The sun will be going down soon, and my team decides to drift alongside the other team's empty Zodiac. I'm relaxing, leaning comfortably against the inflatable's warm rubber pontoon, when Jean-Michel erupts from the water shouting excitedly, "The orcas are eating sharks!"

Three sets of hands lunge for dive masks as we rush to peer anxiously over the side. Beneath us, we see a twenty-eight-foot-long orca swimming toward the other team with an eight-foot-long reef shark dangling in its massive jaws. We hear cartilage crunching as the killer whale consumes the whole shark in three gigantic bites. Quietly, so as not to disturb the incredible action below, I take a breath and slip into the warm water.

I cannot approach the action for fear of accidentally getting into the frame of the other team's cameras. As the surrounding water grows darker with the setting sun, we watch the orcas eat three more sharks. We do not see them catching the sharks. The killer whales hang vertically suspended just beneath the surface. Facing downward, they wait patiently without any movement. It is the classic posture of a hunter. I believe they are echo-locating to sense where the sharks are trying to hide; then, abruptly, they torpedo downward at warp speed. A minute or two later, they ascend with the sharks thrashing in their powerful jaws.

It is amazing that the whales are purposefully returning to us to eat their prey. Why? Is this like a cat who proudly displays a caught mouse? Or are we a source of entertainment while they eat their meal? Watching the seawater turning red from the killer whales' feeding frenzy, I can't help wondering if they aren't considering us for the dessert tray.

As the sun disappears below the horizon, its warm light fades and the water darkens. Unable to film in the submarine twilight, and probably propelled by fears augmented by the dark shadowy water, Jean-Michel's team returns gratefully to the surface.

Instead of rushing back to the *Alcyone*, we take a few minutes to drift under the star-filled heavens. Eager hands hold the twin Zodiacs together as we relive the incredible experience. Everyone bubbles with excitement as we share the wonder of seeing the killer whales hunting sharks. Twenty yards away, a black orca fin rises almost five feet out of the dark water. Starlight glistens on the wet black fin as it cuts through the smooth glassy surface, then the whale exhales a cloud of mist into the dark sky and disappears with a powerful flick of its tail.

An hour after sunrise two days later, I watch children running on a white sand beach, casting long shadows from the morning sun. Leaning against a coconut tree, I enjoy seeing them at their play. We are at Pihun Island, our last stop in Papua New Guinea. This little island is unique from all the others. It is the cleanest and the most fair. Just beyond the village, I see a woman sweeping one of the small island's dirt pathways. About me, other villagers are attending to their daily chores; I notice how fit and healthy they look. The general mood that resides here is one of happiness and good will. The answer to all this good fortune, again, lies in the middle of the village.

For a church, the humble building isn't very large. The Seventh-day Adventist missionaries have also built a school here for the children. Just like the young people at Wuvalo, these island children are also learning about the world beyond their primitive village. However, instead of false hopes built around Hollywood dreams, these kids are being prepared to face the modern world with a foundation in studies like math, reading, history, music, and the Bible. From inside the church, I hear a slightly out-of-tune choir of young voices offering a song to their Maker.

One of the wonders of Christian missionary work is that some of these island kids will get the opportunity to attend advanced studies at far-off colleges and universities. Becoming doctors, teachers, and pastors, they can return to Papua New Guinea to contribute to the quality of life for all the people here. They are the foundation of hope for this little island nation.

> For wisdom will enter your heart, and knowledge will be pleasant to your soul. Discretion will protect you, and understanding will guard you. (Prov. 2:10-11)

In the distance, I hear the captain sounding the *Alcyone's* horn. It is the call to return to the wind ship. With the noon tide we are sailing for Australia, where I will catch a flight home. Brushing the sand of Papua New Guinea from my clothes, it is with great anticipation that I push the Zodiac out into the water. I will be seeing Cindy in just over a week, and I am planning to ask her to marry me.

> **It is not faith and works; it is not faith or works; it is faith that works.**
> **—Anonymous**

Eighteen

But the fruit of the Spirit is love, joy, peace, patience, kindness, goodness, faithfulness, gentleness and self-control.
—Galatians 5:22-23

Barely a month later, I am sitting at my desk in the basement of the Cousteau Society office in Hollywood. It is late in the afternoon, and I am looking forward to picking Cindy up at the airport. My good mood is slightly tainted with the fact that I haven't yet worked up the courage to ask her to marry me. I am pondering this problem when the telephone rings.

"Steve, this is Dr. Clague, the volcanologist at the Hawaiian Volcano Observatory." He is bubbling with enthusiasm. "A new lava flow is heading for the ocean. If you can get out here right away, you will have ideal diving conditions for the next couple of days."

Excited about another opportunity to capture the underwater lava footage, yet with a sinking heart about the prospects for my date with Cindy, I carry the news upstairs to Jean-Michel Cousteau.

"Wonderful," exclaims Jean-Michel eagerly. "How fast can you reassemble the team?"

I think about Cindy arriving at the airport. Trying to sound disappointed, I say, "Well, everyone's still on vacation from the Papua New Guinea expedition. It will take at least a few days to call them all back."

Jean-Michel leans back in his chair and lightly tugs at his beard—this is not a good sign. He is thinking of alternatives. Grabbing his notebook, he makes a quick telephone call to Bob Talbot, the cameraman who landed on the back of the great white shark in Australia.

"Hello, Bob." Jean-Michel gets right to the point. "How would you like to film lava flowing underwater in Hawaii?" I see my boss beaming as he gets an affirmative answer. "Good. Look, I don't have time right now for details. Just get your equipment together. You'll leave with Steve tomorrow from LAX."

Hanging up the telephone, Jean-Michel grins triumphantly at me. "Bob is bringing his assistance, so now you only need one more person to act as a safety diver." At that moment, David Brown walks nonchalantly into the office. He is a lecturer for the Cousteau Society. He has a simple question about a speaking date, but Jean-Michel interrupts him. "David, how would you like to go diving in Hawaii with Steve?"

David is, of course, ecstatic. "When are we leaving?" he asks enthusiastically.

"Tomorrow," answers Jean-Michel as he picks up the telephone again, already moving on to other problems. "Steve will give you the details."

As I head unhappily for the door, I try my last hope for my evaporating date with Cindy. "Uh, Jean-Michel," I say weakly. "Cindy's arriving tonight."

Jean-Michel looks up and chuckles, "She can help you pack."

I nod, "That's what you said last time."

Jean-Michel happily acknowledges my statement, his mood improved by my discomfort. "I know," he says. "It must be good advice."

Closing the door behind me, David fires his first question. "Are we going to dive with the humpback whales?"

"How do you feel about swimming with lava?" I answer, leaving a stunned David Brown standing slack-jawed in my wake.

David is busy in the basement packing up equipment with several other helpers as I head off to meet Cindy with the bad news.

When she steps off the airplane, I'm waiting with a big bunch of roses. She buries her face in them, inhaling deeply. "Is this because you love me?" she asks happily.

"Well . . . ," I answer, pausing for time, "Yes and no."

Cindy lowers the flowers to her side. Momentarily, I wonder if she isn't freeing up her slugging hand. "You're leaving on another adventure, aren't you?"

"Hawaii, to dive with the lava," I answer meekly. "I just found out an hour ago."

"Tell me you're flying out tomorrow morning." I notice that her hand is clenching into a fist.

"Well, actually, I don't have to leave until the afternoon," I offer lamely, retreating half a step out of slugging range.

Cindy notices my slightly defensive posture. "It's OK," Cindy says soberly. "I never hit a date who brings me roses."

Instead of going directly to the Cousteau Society office, I instead head for the hills above Los Angeles.

"Where are we going?" Cindy asks. I can tell she is still upset but trying her best to deal with it.

"The Los Angeles Observatory," I answer, attempting to sound calm about the important decision I am secretly making.

"Why?" Cindy's curiosity is kicking into high gear.

"I want to show you something before I leave," I answer, being purposefully evasive.

Cindy's look is deep and penetrating. I can see she wants to ask more questions; instead, she places her hand on mine and simply says, "OK."

An hour later we arrive at the observatory. Getting out of the car, I take Cindy down a wooded trail. She is still carrying her flowers, which have gained a ladybug stowaway. Cindy is enjoying the short walk. Having grown up in the mountains of northern California, she loves being in the woods. Hand-in-hand, we arrive five minutes later at a promontory overlooking Los Angeles. Beneath us, the twinkling lights of the vast city sprawl as far as the eye can see. The broad freeways pulsate with swiftly moving ribbons of red and white light, while vibrant neon signs define the borders of the darker city streets. At the center of the huge megalopolis, as if rising above a shimmering ocean of light, stand the glass skyscrapers. The towering buildings glisten with inner and reflected radiance, like windows into a futuristic world.

"It's beautiful!" exclaims Cindy.

I look at the excitement and happiness shining in her eyes. Holding the roses in one hand, she places her other hand in mine. I know she wants me to kiss her; instead, I ask Cindy to marry me.

"What!"

"I said, will you marry me?" The suspense is more nerve-racking than diving with great white sharks.

"Of course, I'll marry you, Stephen." Cindy punctuates her statement with a light kiss. "But this doesn't get you off the hook for leaving me behind when you're going off on another adventure."

"That's why I brought you up here." I nod at the glowing metropolis beneath us. "Life is so huge and full of mystery. I want to explore the wonders of this world and to chase after dreams. But, more importantly, I want to do these things with you. All of my adventures are only half the fun when you aren't there to be a part of them."

Despite the urgency to pack, we instead sit on the promontory with stars above us and city lights at our feet, making plans for a future where dreams, adventure, and happiness are shared equally.

Thirty-eight hours later, the small Cousteau flying team stands nervously at the stern of the *Tsunami*. We are at the eastern edge of the lava flow. West of us, it looks just as out of control as it did before. However, at this location, the lava is flowing into the ocean at a single point. It means our approach will be a little bit safer.

Leaping into the hot water, we quickly swim downward, leveling off at thirty feet. The water is slightly cooler than before, around eighty degrees Fahrenheit. Again, we are surrounded by the pounding sound of underwater explosions punctuated by the deep rumble of submarine landslides. Huddled in a tight group, we swim toward the loudest of the sounds. The water darkens as we near the shoreline, then we see a faint red glow radiating up from the darkness below us. Triggering his cinema camera, Bob Talbot leads the way with me hovering at his side. Like a black curtain opening, the surging water abruptly clears before us, revealing a thick lava tube weaving its way down the steep shelf like a giant, angry, red worm.

While Bob films, intently focused on the slowly moving lava in front of him, I watch other lava worms weaving their way toward us. Gently taking Bob's elbow, I squeeze a warning when one gets too close. Reacting instantly, Bob shifts the camera lens to capture the tube as it drops over a shelf, slowly spilling tons of molten rock.

Twenty minutes later, with the camera empty, we beat a hasty retreat back to the *Tsunami*. Heading back to the boat launch, everyone is in high spirits. Our excitement lasts all the way back to the hotel, until Bob opens the underwater cinema camera and, instead of film, discovers confetti. The complex threading system inside the high-speed thirty-five millimeter camera slipped a cog. Instantly, the sharp-edged gears chewed all our prize footage to shreds.

The following morning, we again prepare to jump into the frothy water from the stern of the *Tsunami*. Staring at the shoreline, I see that the lava flow has increased dramatically. What was a stream of flowing lava yesterday is now a river of cascading, molten rock. It is pouring into the water in a broad, fiery sheet, a liquid avalanche of flowing stone. Jumping into the hot water and swimming quickly downward, we discover that the water is much warmer at the thirty-foot level.

Determined to recapture the lost footage, we swim vigorously toward the shoreline. The bombardment of underwater sound and shock waves intensifies. When we see the steep slope of the bottom through black clouds of swirling debris, I turn and signal Bob's assistant and David Brown to maintain a position well above us. Splitting the team into two buddy pairs gives us a safety backup should anything go wrong.

Swimming in toward the steep, rocky shelf, we film unstable lava rubble. Smoking, lava boulders tumble down the forty-five degree incline of the shelf. Abruptly, a large area begins to slide, quickly becoming a minor avalanche that plunges and rumbles loudly into the dark depths below. Carefully moving in closer to capture the dramatic footage, a huge smoking boulder narrowly misses Bob and me. It comes tumbling down from above us without warning, fully two yards in diameter. Weeping jets of steam and laced with red, fiery cracks, it looks like a falling meteorite burning its way through a fluid atmosphere. It bounces between us then somersaults over the shelf, disappearing into the deep blackness below. A wisp of debris floating in the water slowly dissipates in the wake of its passage.

About us, the water visibility keeps changing, going from six to twenty feet, then back to six. It is very disorienting being swept back and forth by surging underwater currents created by the surf above us. Then, we see a faint glimmer of red glowing at a depth of sixty feet. Swimming cautiously downward, we discover a large lava tube—fully a yard in diameter. It momentarily stops its downward plunge. A black crust begins to form, then the leading edge of the tube starts to bulge. The crust suddenly cracks and splits open like an alien egg hatching; then, a cascade of molten rock spills forth in a glorious fountain of liquid fire.

Following the weaving tube downward at the rate of a half-foot every second, we stop our descent at ninety feet. The seawater, making sudden contact with the superhot lava, causes implosions and explosions that send out bone-rattling shock waves. The concussions are so strong that they visibly move the dive masks against our faces. The increased water pressure at this depth magnifies the shock waves to a painful level. As the camera empties its film load, we beat a fast retreat back to the *Tsunami*.

Returning to the hotel, we are ecstatic to discover the film intact inside the camera. Our celebration is only dampened by the intense sinus headaches we are suffering, caused by the violent, underwater shock waves.

Over the next couple of weeks, we have many spectacular days of diving with the molten lava. However, it is our final dive that proves to be almost fatal. Bob and I are filming a pair of lava tubes at a depth of eighty feet when we are hit by a powerful shock wave. It slams against our bodies, completely rattling us; then, from beneath us, comes the heavy rolling sound of a massive avalanche. A deep black cloud of debris swirls up from the depths, engulfing us in absolute darkness mixed with sweltering heat. Bob and I reach out and clutch each other just as we are struck by a tremendous undertow of surging water. The downward plunging current hurls us tumbling and spinning in complete darkness toward the depths below.

Swimming with all our might against the powerful downward pull, we break free of the current, only to find ourselves lost in deep darkness, not knowing which way is up or down. Sensing the changing water pressure against our dive masks as our only guide, it takes three long minutes to struggle back to clearer water. Thankfully reuniting with the other diver pair, I check my depth gauge. I am astounded to discover that the undertow pulled us down to a depth of 135 feet. After allowing a few extra minutes in the water for decompression, we quickly return to Russell's boat.

Pulling off my steaming wet suit, I look toward the fiery tempest raging at the shoreline. The massive lava flow continues to grow more dangerous on a daily basis. I realize it is time to end this expedition. With thoughts of Cindy filling my mind, I turn to the divers and thankfully say, "Pack up. We're going home."

There is no greater challenge than to surpass yourself.

Nineteen

Fangs for the Memories
by Margery Spielman

All are parts of one stupendous whole, whose body nature is and God, the soul.

—Alexander Pope

Oscar has a grin that a vampire would envy. Imagine fangs on a four-foot torpedo that launches itself toward anyone who jumps in the water! We're like goldfish trapped in an aquarium with a piranha, except in this case, the aquarium is the Caribbean Ocean, the goldfish are Olympic swimmers and professional scuba divers, and the piranha is a barracuda named Oscar, whose territory we have just invaded.

We are fifty miles at sea, anchored at a place called the White Sand Ridge. The nearest landfall is the west end of Grand Bahamas Island, lying well out of sight to the southeast. Twenty of us are together for two weeks aboard an eighty-five-foot catamaran named *Bottom Time II*.

The anchor is twenty feet below, resting on a flat sandy bottom that extends outward for more than forty miles. Because the white sand reflects sunlight, the sea's surface is luminous, almost iridescent. Leaning against the railing, I am dazzled by the sparkling expanse of emeralds and aquamarines that shimmer into the distance.

My legs move with the ship's twin hulls, pitching and rolling to the rhythm of rippling waves. Peering overboard into the crystal-clear water, I trace the outlines of a sunken wreck, strewn haphazardly across the bottom. It's not a Spanish galleon laden with gold, but a glorified junk pile.

The tangled debris was once a beacon light. Supported high off the water on stanchions, it warned navigators to watch for dangerous shoals. Now the rusted beams support something else. After years of submersion, they have become encrusted with colonies of bright corals and anemones. Vibrant clusters of tentacles wave in the currents like blossoms in a breeze. Providing food and shelter, the coral gardens have attracted a wealth of other creatures.

Rainbow-colored reef fishes forage inside coral crevices. Giant stingrays tuck themselves under the sand, while schools of jacks and mullets spiral over the bottom like living whirlwinds. The wreck is a rich oasis in the subsea desert, whose treasure is not gold, but life.

This enormous sand bank is also the playground of a remarkable pod of Atlantic spotted dolphins, whose members are renowned for their friendly interactions with human visitors. Free and untamed, these individuals live according to their own agendas. We do not bribe them with food, nor try to control them in any way. Out here, the dolphins are in charge. It is like a zoo in reverse: human captives pacing the decks of their floating pens, waiting for the animals to come and visit.

The primary goal of our expedition is to introduce the Olympic swimmers to the dolphins and to capture the encounters on film. Now we have a secondary goal: getting past Oscar. He guards the wreck like a dragon guards treasure. It's impossible to sneak into the water without him zooming in for a close inspection. Since great barracudas are known to be territorial, I suppose this one is justified in sticking his nose into everyone's business. Nevertheless, we do not appreciate his fangs anywhere near our body parts.

Now that we have met Oscar, and lived to tell the tale, we scout the horizon for any sign of a dorsal fin. Suddenly, someone on deck yells, "Dolphins!" The ship explodes into a blur of bodies, moving at warp speed as if to battle stations. Ripping off T-shirts, we stampede to the lower deck, which is already a mad scramble of hands grabbing equipment, fins flip-flopping, and sunglasses flying. Twenty crazed humans peel off into the water like navy commandos. We must be quite a sight for the dolphins. As for Oscar, he has more sense than to stick around a human feeding-frenzy.

Five frisky dolphins welcome us, winding their way through a maze of arms and legs. We take turns diving with whichever dolphin comes closest. They seem to enjoy mimicking our movements—diving when we dive, twirling when we twirl, and rocketing to the surface with us when we run out of air. Everyone is careful not to touch them unless the animals themselves initiate contact. Although dolphins are extremely tactile with each other, most do not appreciate being handled by humans. Offenders are usually given a wide berth, and it takes a long time to earn back their trust.

When the dolphins discover our Olympic swimmers, they dash in circles like excited puppies, bubbles streaming from their blowholes. Focusing beams of sound and projecting them into the water in a series of high-pitched clicks and whistles, they summon others within sonar range.

Soon we are surrounded by the whole neighborhood. Spotted dolphins begin arriving in small groups from every direction. The older individuals have more markings than the younger ones. Elders are entirely covered—white spots on top and black ones underneath. Juveniles have only splatterings on their sides and bellies, and young calves have no marks at all. Now there are as many dolphins as there are humans, splashing and diving together in one gigantic, fantastic pool party.

Warm and clear, the Caribbean Ocean is like a swimming pool without sides. The shallow bottom is within our breath-holding capacity, so we don't need to use scuba. Besides, the dolphins seem spooked by the exhalation bubbles. Free-diving feels more natural; surfacing for air like marine mammals seems more in tune with the environment.

Matt Biondi, owner of eight Olympic gold medals, is incredible to watch. At six feet, seven inches tall, Matt is ten feet long with his arms outstretched. That's longer than the seven-foot dolphins! Demonstrating his speed and agility, he draws an excited crowd of juveniles who wheel around him, nodding their heads and whistling in approval.

Equally impressive are Tracie Ruiz-Conforto and the Josephson twins, Karen and Sarah—all three are gold medalists in synchronized swimming. The twins, with a lifetime of practice together, move in perfect harmony, amazing everyone with their breath-holding skills. Twisting and twirling with dolphin partners, they perform a stunning underwater ballet.

Tracie is the mermaid in our midst. She's just like a dolphin, moving in fluid elegance. Holding her breath for minutes at a time, she surfaces, takes a deep breath, and goes immediately back underwater. Meanwhile, the rest of us are gasping for air between dives. Tracie is truly the most graceful person I have ever seen underwater. Happily, I'm not the only one who is overwhelmed by our champions. Whereas most dolphin encounters range from ten to sixty minutes, our very first one lasts a record three hours.

Toward the end of the session, as I'm resting on the surface, a young female dolphin brushes up against my shoulder, her face just a few inches away. Resisting the urge to touch her, I keep my hands glued to my sides and softly coo through my snorkel. "You're so beautiful," I whisper, my heart filled with emotion. A soft brown eye, brimming with intelligence, peers inquisitively into my mask. Every time I vocalize, she squints as if trying to see inside of me. It feels as if we're both asking each other simultaneously, Who are you?

Like two different worlds converging, I recognize in her an aquatic version of myself. We're separate species, yet we share the same sense of joy, curiosity, and trust. Looking into her radiant eye, I feel an enormously powerful connection. I think she feels it, too. For several moments we experience the magic of two spirits spilling into each other, then the spell is broken and we burst into one last playful romp beneath the waves.

A wonderful week passes, with multiple daily encounters— but not today. Today, we have had nothing. It's four o'clock in the afternoon. There is no wind, and the tropical sun is scorching. The humidity is high enough to hatch mosquitoes. Everyone is irritable from the heat.

Naturally, the last person I want to deal with right now is Donna—or should I say Prima Donna? She is seventeen years old, an Olympic hopeful, surly and ill-mannered. From the moment we departed, Donna has been acting like Cleopatra, treating the scuba divers on board as if we were ship rats. The irony here is that most of the swimmers went on this trip free of charge because the divers paid full price in order to help sponsor them.

Now, Her Majesty is directly in my face, decreeing that "only swimmers and not divers should be allowed in the water with the dolphins." Suddenly, I'm Chernobyl, ready to explode! I feel like throwing her overboard to Oscar but decide to throw myself instead. While most of the crew members are down below in their air-conditioned quarters, I slather on sunscreen, grab mask, fins, and snorkel and jump ship.

The fiberglass cave between the ship's twin hulls is enticing. I venture inside, welcoming the shade and privacy. Then I discover I am not alone. Suspended three feet below and four feet in front of me is Oscar. Motionlessly, we eyeball each other. Should I withdraw graciously? The cool and quiet is so refreshing I hate to leave. After all, the barracuda hasn't actually chewed up anybody, I rationalize.

Suddenly, the fish starts snapping his jaws together like an attack dog. I begin nervously back-pedaling, wishing I could walk on water. Then something catches my eye. Oscar has a hitchhiker—a small fish, several inches long, known as a remora or sharksucker. This little fellow seems to be grooming him. As the barracuda thrusts his mouth open, the gill openings on the side of his head extend, enabling the slender fish to slip inside. It darts under the bony cover, snatches up a buglike parasite and zips out before the hatch closes.

I watch in awe as the process repeats itself. Suddenly, it becomes clear. Oscar's vicious dog routine isn't a strike warning at all—it's his personal hygiene! Intrigued by my new discovery, I ease in for a better view, but my sudden movement startles him. He swims out from under the boat. Wondering what else goes on in a barracuda's world, I gulp a breath of air and glide under the hull after him. For the next three-and-a-half hours, I am Oscar's shadow.

First, we tour his domain. He shows me the perimeters, swimming a wide circle around the wreck; then, he cruises down among his subjects, whom I expect to see dash for cover. Instead, hundreds of tiny silversides, in a huge welcoming committee, rise up as one to greet him. With tail fins pumping to keep up, they seem delighted by the big fish's presence. I can almost hear little munchkin voices squealing, "Look! It's Oscar! Oscar, wait for us!"

Eventually all of the little fish give up, and everyone swims back down to the safety of the wreck—all except one. One small silverside has dropped out of school to swim with Godzilla! Not only puzzling, the picture of these two unlikely sidekicks is quite comical.

Several hours have passed and now Oscar and I swim side-by-side, our heads only a foot apart. The distance between us has shrunk dramatically, and not just in the physical sense. I begin to realize that fear is about not understanding. When you don't understand someone, it is easy to misconstrue his behavior. I know now that Oscar is not the bully I thought he was—he's just a curious and tenacious creature, trying to survive in a fish-eat-fish world. The monster is not a monster anymore.

Suddenly, I have this ridiculous urge to pet him. I look fondly at my fingers, wondering how I would manage without them. Pet a barracuda? No, I cannot believe I'm entertaining such a stupid idea—but then, before I can stop myself—I boldly go where no one in their right mind has gone before!

With at least some sensibilities still intact, I start at a point farthest away from Oscar's teeth. Taking a deep breath, I begin caressing his tail fin more lightly than a butterfly kiss. He quivers slightly at my touch, but doesn't seem to mind. Encouraged, I try again, only this time I pet him farther forward along his side. I stroke him several more times until I finally have to stop to clear my mask. No wonder it's full of water—I'm grinning like a Cheshire cat!

Meanwhile, topside, I am the one who is being observed. Totally focused on the fish, I am completely unaware that people are watching me. The realization hits home when Donna, the queen of the Nile, graces the water. Immediately Oscar rushes in, with me trailing behind. Madly thrashing her arms and legs, Donna shrieks in the whiniest of voices, "Get your stupid fish away from me!" I shake my head in disbelief, laughing at the absurdity, yet, secretly, for a wicked moment, I wish Oscar really was under my command!

Now, it's almost sunset and several other barracudas, smaller than Oscar, trespass his territory. My diving buddy is visibly unnerved by the intruders, yet as long as they don't turn their noses toward him, he tolerates their presence. Then, I notice the little sharksucker clamping down on the big fish's head. Is he securing for takeoff? Sure enough, one of the barracudas has challenged Oscar, who blasts off in pursuit like a guided missile.

I had no idea a fish could move that fast! One minute he is beside me and the next he's gone! Squinting after him, I see nothing but deepening gloom. I feel as if part of me has been ripped away. After all of these hours of communing with another life form—and then to have it suddenly disappear—I feel abandoned. The truth is, I've grown attached to this orthodontic nightmare!

Lifting my head from the water, I catch the splendid remains of a tropical sunset—pinks and mauves in every hue imaginable. I marvel at the beauty and mystery of life and how little of it we really comprehend—like Oscar. He seemed so repulsive until I got to know him. I pity the person who would try to catch him now. I'd be furious! I remember Captain Cousteau saying, "People protect what they love."

Then, I think of Donna. Perhaps if I had spent over three hours alone with her, she wouldn't seem so repulsive either. For a moment, I am stunned by the revelation. Maybe that's the lesson the old fish was teaching me.

Putting my head back in the water, intending to snorkel to the boat, I nearly jump out of my skin. There's Oscar, right next to me. "I can't believe you came back," I sputter. At the same moment, I realize how late I am for dinner. "Sorry, old buddy, now it's my turn to leave," I tell him, kicking toward the stern. Halfway back, trickles of water start seeping into my mask again. Looking over at Oscar, I can't stop smiling. Here

I am, in the middle of the ocean, being escorted home by a fish! Suddenly, the image of the little silverside pops into my mind. I suppose a human and a barracuda make an odd-looking couple, too.

We arrive at the swim-step, and I remove my fins. "Goodnight, Oscar, see you tomorrow," I say, climbing up the ladder. I feel so honored that already on this trip, I have twice connected with another species. Maybe Donna will be the third, I muse, grabbing my towel.

During dinner, my friends on board tease me about my "new boyfriend." "No, I did not kiss him goodnight," I reply jokingly. A spirit of camaraderie has replaced the earlier tensions of the day. I look across the room at Donna and smile. Indirectly, she's responsible for my wonderful afternoon.

Tomorrow, filmmaker Tom Fitz plans to shoot a sequence of me with Oscar. He hopes to use it in his current video featuring the swimmers and dolphins. After finishing dinner, he asks me, "Why don't you tell us about your day with Oscar."

When I explain the real reason why the barracuda snaps his teeth together, everyone laughs in collective relief. One more time, I am amazed how a little bit of knowledge can lead to understanding, and how understanding can lead to compassion.

The lesson is even more obvious the next day when Oscar, between our dolphin encounters, manages to entertain a whole flotilla of curious new friends.

No longer can we discount the lives of sensitive and intelligent creatures merely because they assume non-human form. The things that make life most precious and blessed—courage and daring, conscience and compassion, imagination and originality, fantasy and play—do not belong to our kind alone.

—Gary Kowalski

Twenty

Love is patient, love is kind. It does not envy, it does not boast, it is not proud. It is not rude, it is not self-seeking, it is not easily angered, it keeps no record of wrongs. Love does not delight in evil but rejoices with the truth. It always protects, always trusts, always hopes, always perseveres.

—1 Corinthians 13:4-7

I am waiting nervously next to an altar covered with wild flowers. It is the most exciting day of my life. Standing at my side, Jean-Michel Cousteau is very handsome in his tuxedo. He places a hand on my shoulder and quietly confides, "Not too late to send you dashing off on an expedition to some remote location."

I grin at him, too full of emotion to say anything witty in return. The piano begins to play "Cannon in D," as the rest of the wedding party starts their slow march down the aisle. I see my friend Sam walking at the lead. He grins broadly but, for an instant, I remember his sorrow and guilt when he got caught up in the darker intrigues described in my book *Journey into Darkness*. The bad experience, brought on because of marijuana use, almost cost him his freedom—and could have violently ended his life. At his side walks my wife's best friend, Dagmar. In three years she will give birth to a wonderful son, but her joy will be short when cancer takes her in 1995. Next comes Margery Spielman, the person who has been my friend the longest. Together, Margery and I have known great happiness and faced many tragedies. For three long years the only way she could visit me was in a federal prison. Proudly walking with her is my big brother Jim. I would lose him in the summer of 1994 to a sudden and tragic death. I usually remember him best during happy moments because our laughs are identical. It is when my laughter comes forward irresistibly—loud and uncontrollable—that I hear echoes of Jim coming from within me; then, for a moment, the happiness is usually shattered.

At this moment, I do not know the tragedies that lurk in the near future. Instead, I see Cindy in her flowing gown and cannot believe this beautiful woman, my best friend, is about to become my wife. At the altar, we link hands and just before the ceremony begins, we pause to look at all our guests gathered in the small church. I see our families, a wealth of friends, and many expedition companions from The Cousteau Society. With each group of faces flashes a flood of memories: childhood hopes and dreams with my family, happy adventures with my friends, and the challenges of expedition life with my Cousteau companions. Then, I turn to face Cindy. In her smiling eyes I see a future yet to be, made of dreams, hopes, and aspirations. Yet, we will also reap a full measure of tragedy and sadness. All of this is simply part of life. In this instant of time, Cindy and I link hands and become lifelong companions. Whatever the future bears, we will face it together. I will be at her side for the birth of our two little girls, and only yesterday, I stood with her as the doctor who delivered Cindy was laid to rest.

If there is anything I have learned about life, it is that all of us will face wonder and tragedy; we will know love and hatred, success and failure. Life is a relentless cascade of positives and negatives. To have the strength and courage to face all that life is hurling at us takes the fortitude of family and friends. None of us can stand alone, which leads us to the most important decision any of us can make: simply to invite the best friend of all humankind, Jesus Christ, into our lives.

> I have told you these things, so that in me you may have peace. In this world you will have trouble. But take heart! I have overcome the world. (John 16:33)

After the ceremony, we gather at my mother's house to celebrate. It is there that Jean-Michel reveals his plans for us—with a toast. "Cindy, I wish you the greatest happiness in life. I hope your honeymoon is full of joy, wonder, and whispers of dreams yet to be. However, right after your honeymoon, I need to send Steve to dive with great white sharks in Australia." Before the surprise of this news can sink in, Jean-Michel takes Cindy's hand and asks, "While Steve is gone, do you think you can take a couple of weeks off from school?"

"Why?" Cindy has no idea what is coming next.

"Because I need for you to join the first team of women Cousteau divers," laughs Jean-Michel, completely pleased at the shock on Cindy's face.

Cindy is utterly speechless, so Jean-Michel continues his surprise by weaving Margery into it, too. "I want to film you and Margery Spielman swimming with Atlantic-spotted dolphins in the Bahamas."

> Surely goodness and love will follow me all the days of my life, and I will dwell in the house of the LORD forever. (Psalm 23:6)

To be continued . . .

Publisher's note: To contact the author regarding Christian motivational presentations or public school drug educational programs, please write:

Stephen Arrington
P.O. Box 3234
Paradise, CA 95967

Author's Note

How rare and wonderful is that flash of a moment when we realize we have discovered a friend.

—William Rotsler

Real friends are rare treasures that enhance all the positive aspects of our lives. Friends help us to put our fears into perspective. Friends applaud our successes and lend a supporting shoulder for our failures. Happiness is built on the foundation of true friendships; therefore, it is with great pleasure that I introduce one of my very best friends, the author of chapter 19 and the illustrator for this book.

Margery Spielman is an internationally recognized marine and environmental artist, lecturer, naturalist, and professional diver. Described as a visionary artist, she exhibits her watercolor paintings in major marine art exhibitions, including those in Maui, Kauai, Santa Barbara, and Paris. A member of the Screen Actors Guild, she has worked underwater on numerous television and film productions as a stunt diver, model, actor, and production manager. Involved with The Cousteau Society since 1976, her free-lance assignments include expedition research and logistics, expedition diving, slide and lecture presentations, and illustrations for publication. Captain Jacques-Yves Cousteau displays one of her paintings in the dining salon aboard the Alcyone.

> Margery Spielman is a philosophical artist,
> whose work reflects life's interconnections. Her
> paintings are visual adventures—the longer you
> explore them, the more you discover.
> —Jean-Michel Cousteau

Margery is directly responsible for my coming to the attention of Jean-Michel Cousteau. It is because of her help and glowing recommendations that I got the opportunity to dive for The Cousteau Society. I am greatly pleased that she has agreed to be a contributing writer and illustrator for this book series.

Note: for information on obtaining Margery Spielman's artwork (lithographs, greeting cards, paintings, etc.), write to her at P.O. Box 98, Ventura, CA 93001.

We welcome comments from our readers. Feel free to write to us at the following address:

Editorial Department
Huntington House Publishers
P.O. Box 53788
Lafayette, LA 70505

More Good Books from Huntington House

Journey into Darkness: Nowhere to Land
by Stephen L. Arrington

This story begins on Hawaii's glistening sands and ends in the mysterious deep with the Great White shark. In between, the author finds himself trapped in the drug smuggling trade—unwittingly becoming the "Fall Guy" in the highly publicized John Z. DeLorean drug case. Naval career shattered, his youthful innocence tested, and friends and family put to the test of loyalty, Arrington locks onto one truth during his savage stay in prison and endeavors to share that critical truth now. Focusing on a single important message to young people—to stay away from drugs—the author recounts his horrifying prison experience and allows the reader to take a peek at the source of hope and courage that helped him survive.

ISBN 1-56384-003-3

High on Adventure:
Stories of Good, Clean,
Spine-tingling Fun
by Stephen L. Arrington

In the first volume of this exciting series of adventure stories, you'll meet a seventeen-and-a-half-foot Great White shark face-to-face, dive from an airplane toward the earth's surface at 140 M.P.H., and explore a sunken battle cruiser from World War II in the dark depths of the South Pacific Ocean. Author and adventurer Stephen Arrington tells many exciting tales from his life as a navy frogman and chief diver for The Cousteau Society, lacing each story with his Christian belief and outlook that life is an adventure waiting to be had.

ISBN 1-56384-082-0

Do Angels Really Exist?
Separating Fact from Fantasy
by Dr. David O. Dykes

Have you ever seen an angel? Don't be too quick to answer "no." For most of us, angels evoke images of graceful winged, white figures. But, according to the Bible, angels are God's armored warriors ready to protect His kingdom in heaven, as well as His beloved followers on earth. By citing dozens of fascinating angel encounters, the author presents evidence that angels roam the earth today. You might be encountering angels without even knowing it.

ISBN 1-56384-105-3

In His Majesty's Service:
Christians in Politics
by Robert A. Peterson

In His Majesty's Service is more than a book about politics. It's a look at how real men have worked out their Christian beliefs in the rough-and-tumble world of high-level government, war, and nation building. From these fascinating portraits of great Western leaders of the past, we can discover how to deal with some of the most pressing problems we face today. This exciting, but historically accurate, volume is as entertaining as it is enlightening.

ISBN 1-56384-100-2

ORDER THESE HUNTINGTON HOUSE BOOKS

- *Anyone Can Homeschool*—Terry Dorian, Ph.D. & Zan Peters Tyler
- *The Assault*—Dale A. Berryhill
- *Basic Steps to Successful Homeschooling*—Vicki Brady
- *Beyond Political Correctness*—David Thibodaux, Ph.D.
- *The Best of HUMAN EVENTS*—Edited by James C. Roberts
- *Bleeding Hearts and Propaganda*—James R. Spencer
- *Circle of Death*—Richmond Odom
- *Children No More*—Brenda Scott
- *Combat Ready*—Lynn Stanley
- *Conquering the Culture*—David Eich
- *The Culture War in America*—Bob Rosio
- *The Dark Side of Freemasonry*—Ed Decker
- *The Demonic Roots of Globalism*—Gary Kah
- *Do Angels Really Exist?*—Dr. David O. Dykes
- *En Route to Global Occupation*—Gary Kah
- *Everyday Evangelism*—Ray Comfort
- *From Earthquakes to Global Unity*—Paul McGuire
- *Getting Out: An Escape Manual for Abused Women*—Kathy Cawthon
- *Global Bondage*—Cliff Kincaid
- *Handouts and Pickpockets*—William Hoar
- *Health Begins in Him*—Terry Dorian, Ph.D.
- *Heresy Hunters*—Jim Spencer
- *High on Adventure*—Stephen Arrington
- *High-Voltage Christianity*—Dr. Michael L. Brown
- *How to Homeschool (Yes, You!)*—Julia Toto
- *Hungry for God*—Larry E. Myers
- *In His Majesty's Service*—Bob Peterson
- *A Jewish Conservative Looks at Pagan America*—Don Feder
- *Journey into Darkness*—Stephen Arrington
- *Kinsey, Sex and Fraud*—Dr. Judith A. Reisman & Edward Eichel
- *The Media Hates Conservatives*—Dale A. Berryhill
- *Nations without God*—Barney Fuller
- *New Gods for a New Age*—Richmond Odom
- *Out of Control*—Brenda Scott
- *Outcome-Based Education*—Peg Luksik & Pamela Hoffecker
- *Parent Police**—Ingrid Guzman
- *Resurrecting the Third Reich*—Richard Terrell
- *The Social Service Gestapo**—Janson Kauser
- *The Truth about False Memory Syndrome*—Dr. James Friesen
- *The Walking Wounded*—Jeremy Reynalds
- *What Do You Do with an Ousted Liberal?*—Merrill Matthews
  & Don Adair

*Available in Salt Series

Available at bookstores everywhere or order direct from:

Huntington House Publishers
P.O. Box 53788 • Lafayette, LA 70505

Call toll-free 1-800-749-4009.